Carpenter Road

A Leighton Jones Book

Also By N.M. Brown

The Girl On The Bus

Praise For N.M. Brown

"Anything but formulaic, the story is well planned and imaginative in its execution. It's also riddled with believable characters whose actions are in keeping with the challenges and their personalities." **Mark Wilson – Author**

"This is a slick, well-written book that will capture your imagination and your heart." Shane Mc Guigan **– Amazon Reviewer**

"WOW!!! This is a five star page turner. I could not put this book down." **Derek – Amazon Reviewer**

"I highly recommend The Girl on the Bus for those looking for a fast, sinister, atmospheric read." **Christine – Goodreads Reviewer**

"Well written, full of tension and suspense this is a story that grabs you from the beginning and does not let up. Highly recommended." **Lee – Goodreads Reviewer**

"OMG where have you been Norman M. Brown because you wore my goose bumps out!" **Susan Hampson – Books From Dusk Till Dawn**

For my children

These events take place ten years before those of The Girl on the Bus.

Prologue

In the hour before her death, Sarah Kline had been squirming at the cluttered table for too long. She had been waiting for almost half an hour for the other members of the dinner party to finally finish eating their various main courses. Only then would she finally be free to excuse herself from the claustrophobic corner of the Beach House Café in the harbour area of Oceanside. The café was a relaxed place where surfers and tourists were equally welcome. On that particular Friday evening, some Sheryl Crowe song was playing in the background and bouncing off the various classic surfboards that were hanging from the ceiling.

All around Sarah people were tearing at burgers that were dripping with guacamole and ranch sauce. She, however, had stupidly skipped the main course, opting only for a side order. Her reason was purely financial – it was close to the end of the month and her bank balance would not extend to a main course and beers. If she had to choose, beer would be given greater priority. She had therefore decided to order something small and cheap.

When the sizzling bowl of hot fries had arrived, Sarah had cheerfully popped each of the golden sticks into her mouth one by one. Upon reflection, she wondered if she should have paced herself a little. Having finished her small bowl of pleasure, Sarah realised that she would have to endure watching her colleagues gradually devour another entire course. This situation would have been okay if she had been sitting beside someone sociable. Unfortunately, Sarah was hemmed in a corner by a mousy woman from the mailroom who smiled nervously, avoiding eye contact with any of the other diners, whilst taking delicate sips of mineral water.

Taking a gulp of her beer, Sarah felt the rush of bubbles tingle her tongue. The sensation reminded her of her childhood, when she had often loved drinking Coke from green glass bottles.

As drank, Sarah glanced absently through the large window of the café at the bruised colours of the darkening October sky. She almost shivered at the thought of standing outside in the cool air. It was not a particularly inviting prospect at this time of night, but her addiction was a powerful force and a means of escape.

Following the imposition of a strict smoking ban in her office – the result of a dangerous fire in a mailroom cupboard – Sarah had promised to quit cigarettes almost three months earlier. At the age of twenty-six she had better things than cigarettes to spend her income on; plus, the habit was becoming increasingly antisocial. Unfortunately, wrestling that particular monkey off her back had been much harder than she had anticipated, and now that most of her colleagues had replaced the coffee-break smoke with an extra strong latte, she was forced to visit the stub-littered area outside the depot's fire exit on her own.

The reason for the celebration that evening was Ted Shennan's leaving dinner. He was a popular and good-natured manager, who fostered good relations with the staff, but an unseasonal dip in temperature had meant fewer people than were expected had shown up for his farewell feast. This fact didn't seem to bother Ted, who was laughing loudly and shovelling lobster into his mouth with all the passion of a Roman emperor.

Eventually, Sarah's craving eclipsed her sense of propriety. She stood up, excused herself, and squeezed free of the table and diners.

Her long dark coat was hanging like a witch's cloak on the row of hooks next to the café's entrance. Sarah slipped on the garment and felt a sense of relief as her fingers instinctively found the angular cigarette packet in one of the pockets. Pulling open the door, she glanced quickly at the other diners. For a second, she considered sneaking home without letting anyone know.

'Goodnight!' one of the cheery waiting staff called to her, thinking that she was genuinely leaving.

'I'll be back. I'm just heading out for a smoke,' she replied, but the busy waiter had already been distracted by a waving hand from another table.

It was even colder outside than she'd expected. For most of her life she had only ever known the southern Californian coast to be comfortably warm in October. Yet tonight a formidable bank of fog had drifted in silently from the ocean and was creeping into the harbour area like a sprawling phantom. Having pulled her collar up against the relatively chill air, Sarah plunged one hand into her pocket and pulled out a battered pack of cigarettes. Popping one in her mouth, she felt the pockets for her plastic lighter: both were empty.

'Shit!' Sarah stomped the heel of her shoe against the sidewalk. Her lighter was most likely sitting on her cramped desk – back at the depot.

She glanced over her shoulder to peer through the window at her fellow diners. They were all still consuming their meals; returning to endure another half hour of drooling and slurping was not an option. In a moment of desperation, Sarah briefly considered trying to cross the freeway to either of the two nearby gas stations. However, deciding that she was quite likely to find another shunned smoker at the rear of the café, Sarah wandered to the quieter Cassidy Street side of the building. The parking lot, which was located behind the café, was empty except for an old silver Ford and a chilled-food delivery van.

Sighing, she wandered back to the main entrance, and discovered a woman standing smoking on the corner of Cassidy and the South Coast Highway. Sarah, who was still fixated on a nicotine hit, naturally assumed that the woman was a diner from another table, who had also popped outside for a smoke.

'Excuse me!' Sarah called over to the woman.

'Hey, Jenna.' She responded with a small wave and hurried across the sidewalk to Sarah.

'Did you call me Jenna?' Sarah asked, with a small frown.

'Sorry, I thought you were somebody else.' The woman partly turned her head and blew a grey cone of smoke into the air. 'Did you call to me?'

'I wanted to ask if you could give me a light, please.'

'Sure, honey,' the woman said as she turned around, revealing her leopard-print jacket, stretched miniskirt and cropped vest. She dug into her tiny pink handbag and produced a cheap, gold coloured lighter, which she held out to Sarah.

'Are you a pros …?' the words escaped Sarah's lips before she'd intended them to.

'Yeah, I am,' the woman said defiantly. 'You got something you want to say about that?'

'No,' Sarah said with a shrug. 'I just … guess it's a cool night to be working out here.'

'Damn true, but, take it from me, the weather sure isn't the worst part of the job. Are you wanting this damn thing or not?'

'Sorry,' Sarah said, as she accepted the cheap plastic lighter and lit her cigarette.

At that moment, a glossy black police car pulled into the brightly lit gas station across the freeway. In response to this, the woman instinctively turned away from the vehicle. Her almost subconscious response at seeing the car was not lost on Sarah.

'Do you get much bother from the cops?' she asked, with an air of fascination.

'No, honey,' the woman replied, with a shrug of her shoulders, 'most of the time we're pretty much invisible – not just to the cops either. It's what comes with the territory. But sometimes some assholes from Vice will haul a couple of girls into the station to keep the legitimate business owners happy. The rest of the time, we're just trash on the street.' Something shifted in her eyes, as if a light had dimmed. 'Hookers aren't real people – at least not to the customers, the cops, or the public. Working on the streets is a bit like being a ghost.'

There was a moment of uncomfortable silence until Sarah suddenly realised that she could at least make a gesture of acceptance. She turned to the woman and met her gaze.

'I'm Sarah,' she said, purposefully, and held out her hand.

The woman looked at Sarah's hand and then at her face, as if to say: are you shitting me? But the persistent hand remained, hovering there just the same.

'Rochelle,' she said, taking Sarah's hand and shaking it briefly.

'Your hand's freezing,' Sarah said. 'Aren't you cold?'

'No,' Rochelle said, with a shake of her head, 'the temperature doesn't get to me much anymore. I've just got a full bladder. Either that or I've picked up a urine infection again – another bonus of the job I guess.' She smiled grimly and sucked on her cigarette.

Suddenly, Sarah found that her own job, stacking mail in the depot, wasn't quite as grim as she had thought.

'Hey, why don't you use the bathroom in there?' She nodded over her shoulder to the bustling café.

'You kidding?' Rochelle raised her drawn-on eyebrows at the suggestion. 'Dressed like this, I'd be spotted and thrown out before I'd even reached a cubicle. It's cool; I'll survive.'

Sarah looked at Rochelle for a moment then glanced down at her own knee-length coat.

'Listen, take my coat' she announced suddenly. 'I mean it's long enough, and no one will ever know. Our hair's pretty much the same colour so the staff will probably just think it's me heading back in to re-join the party.'

'You sure?' Rochelle asked in a tone of disbelief. Two acts of courtesy in one night was something she had never encountered before.

'Of course,' Sarah smiled, and had already begun to slip her arms out of her coat.

As the two women exchanged garments, each of them knew that the gesture involved a silent exchange of experiences too.

Sneaking quickly into the brightly lit bathroom of the café, Rochelle almost didn't recognise her reflection in the mirror. Her deep-set eyes looked tired and older than her twenty-two years.

Her addiction had stolen everything from her. She had never really fit in at school – it was always a competition to be either the smartest or the most popular. Rochelle, who was neither, had increasingly found herself hanging around at the graffiti-covered skatepark, instead of attending classes for subjects she hadn't liked or couldn't understand. This colourful, concrete landscape was where she had slid into a pit of a relationship with Billy Spencer. He was six years older than her and had lived off a combination of welfare and whatever he could earn from peddling drugs around the regular teenage haunts. On the day of her seventeenth birthday, Billy had relentlessly pestered Rochelle until she reluctantly shared his crack pipe. After that, they were both high for most of the time during the five years they had stumbled along together. However, the previous summer Billy was arrested, in a drugs operation, outside a local pool hall. He made bail, and, after stopping off at home long enough to dump a bag of white powder and pack a bag of clothes, he promptly vanished. Billy's unplanned departure had left Rochelle with no income, a slum of a home and a formidable drug habit. The slide into working the streets was inevitable.

Her reflection revealed the eyes of the girl she had once been, but nothing else. It was like looking at a young girl wearing the mask of an older, troubled woman.

Before she left the warmth of the bathroom, Rochelle stopped in front of the mirrored wall to apply some cherry lip gloss. It made her look more appealing to the customers and hid her anaemia. However, when she reached into the jacket pocket, she realised that the small metal tin was in the pocket of her own cheap coat, rather than this soft fabric. It was then she remembered that her meagre earnings for the night were also in her own jacket. Rochelle hoped the girl who was wearing it was trustworthy, or she might be down a few bucks.

Stepping outside of the café, Rochelle was suddenly more aware of the biting cold that Sarah had mentioned earlier. She was considering telling her this when she realised, with a sense of panic, that Sarah was no longer there. The street was quiet and empty.

'Shit!' Rochelle kicked at the sidewalk.

Trying to calm her jitters, she turned around and pressed her hand to the window of the café and peered through the glass. The tables inside were full of eager diners, but none of them resembled the girl Rochelle had spoken to. As she stepped back from the breath-steamed glass, a young, male waiter pushed assertively through the café door and approached her.

'Hey, do you mind not pressing your face against the window?'

Normally, Rochelle would have told the guy to take a hike, but she needed him.

'I was just looking for a girl – about my height, wearing a leopard-print jacket. Have you seen her inside at all?'

'No, we don't allow street workers in the café,' he replied proudly, as he turned around and disappeared back inside the bright refuge of the café.

'Screw you!' Rochelle shouted after him.

The situation felt weird to Rochelle. Stepping to the edge of the sidewalk, she peered across the freeway at the two parallel gas stations. Their coldly lit forecourts were deserted, and in the creeping fog they resembled deep-sea stations.

Rochelle decided to check the rear of the buff coloured building, in case Sarah had simply walked off to escape the gaze of all the diners. As she wandered around the corner to the deserted parking lot behind the café, she was struck by the blinding glare of full-beam car headlights. Even though the solitary car was parked several feet away, in one of the six bays, Rochelle could hear the engine rumbling, and behind that was the pulsing sound of repetitive, thumping music. The piercing lights of the car were so harsh that Rochelle held up her hand to shield her eyes and stepped instinctively backwards.

The groaning vehicle lurched angrily toward Rochelle, forcing her to stumble to one side. The car missed her by less than a few inches, after which, it screeched out of the quiet parking lot and onto the fog shrouded freeway.

As the vehicle passed her Rochelle tried to kick out at it, but she was too far away.

'Asshole!' she called out.

Turning around, to see if anyone else had witnessed the spectacle, Rochelle noticed something glinting on the dark ground where the car had been parked. Wandering cautiously over to it, she identified the familiar item immediately.

She crouched down and picked up her cheap, imitation-gold lighter. Turning the item over in her hands, Rochelle discovered that it was still warm.

'Bitch!' Rochelle said, and slipped the small object into the plush pocket of somebody else's coat.

1

The early morning fog had burned away to reveal an unbroken vault of blue sky above Oceanside harbour, which was currently flecked with white gulls, gliding on the fresh sea breeze. Although it looked inviting, the tumbling turquoise surf below them attracted only a smattering of swimmers at this time of year – especially so early in the day.

In general, this was an area of the city that was more popular with sailors and fishermen than with tourists – who mostly preferred the boardwalk and the pier, unless they were booked on a whale-watching trip. The harbour consisted of a long slip area, where boats of various sizes were moored amiably together, their countless masts stretching like long needles into the Southern Californian sky. Watching over the area was a sturdy lighthouse, painted white and red.

In a long parking lot, near to the shore, Leighton Jones struggled to carry both Styrofoam coffee cups and the brown paper bag to where the bulky, black Ford Explorer was parked. His partner, Danny Clark, was leaning on the front of the car, staring wistfully across the neatly moored yachts to the water beyond them, where the waves faded into the horizon. The two officers had worked together for three years, since Danny had started, and were now comfortable in each other's company.

'Here you go, buddy,' Leighton said, as he handed over one of the cups to Danny. In the sky above them, a couple of noisy gulls circled, eagerly anticipating any stray crumbs from the officers' bag.

'Thanks, man.' Danny smiled and lifted the cup to his mouth.

'I feel I should warn you,' Leighton said gravely, 'it's pretty hot. I felt my hands melting as I left the place.'

'It's okay, I can drink it straight out of the pot. They say it's not good for your stomach, but I can't swallow it any other way.'

'Not me,' Leighton said proudly, as he used a fingertip to prise off the lid from his own cup. 'I prefer all beverages at room temperature.'

'Yeah, maybe except for beer,' Danny said with a wry smile.

'Hey, remember I drink at the Rooster, so my beer's usually warm too. Did you hear back from the hospital?' As he spoke, Leighton took a warm doughnut from the paper bag, and handed the remaining two across to his partner.

'Thanks,' Danny nodded, 'they said he's still sedated and that they're running some tests. They still don't know if he'll come round at all. The doctor said that no two strokes are ever quite the same, apparently.'

Leighton bit into his warm doughnut, sipped his coffee, and waited an acceptable amount of time before he stated what he believed to be an obvious point.

'Don't you think you should be up there with him?' he asked tentatively.

'I hate the smell of those places,' Danny said, 'it clings to you.'

'The smell – is that what's really keeping you away?'

Danny frowned and gazed into the distance, where some large cruiser was pulling out of the harbour leaving white snakes of foam in its wake. 'I know I should, Jonesy. It's just well …' He rubbed the back of his neck as he spoke. 'Hell, you know what Gretsch is like.'

'Yes, I do, he's an officious prick,' Leighton nodded and took another sip of coffee, 'but I still think you should be there.'

'C'mon, Jonesy. He said that it would have to be *unpaid* leave, I can't go against him. What if he cans me? I need the money. My old man doesn't have medical insurance, so if Gretsch fires me, both of us are screwed.'

'Relax, Danny. He's only a captain: he doesn't have the authority to *can* anyone.' Leighton narrowed his eyes. 'Think about it. If he did, I would have been shining shoes on Skid Row years ago.'

Danny smiled at the image. 'That's very true. The guy seems to have a particular problem with you. Did you sleep with his wife or something?'

'Are you insane? Do you really think Gretsch could find a wife?' Leighton said, whilst chuckling into his Styrofoam coffee cup.

'Good point,' Danny said, and bit into his crumbling pastry.

'Gretsch just got to where he is today by learning some buzzwords and kissing butt. There are guys like him everywhere – not just in policing. They love to hang out with guys who are just like them, devising high-profile initiatives to keep everyone else busy. I guess that's what makes them feel important and in charge.'

'I can see that's working for him,' Danny smiled.

'Yeah, but here's the problem,' Leighton narrowed his eyes as he spoke, 'the biggest threat to guys like that are any folks who don't kiss butt or use fancy buzzwords – the ones who simply get on with doing their job. Guys like Gretsch don't understand people like us and so they want to get rid of us.'

'Eliminate the threat,' Danny said assertively.

'Exactly!'

'So, is that the speech you're going to give at the podium when he gets made chief?' Danny asked with a half-smile.

'Don't tempt me, partner,' Leighton chuckled. 'Listen,' he said in a softer voice, 'is anyone up at the hospital with your pop just now?'

'There was last night,' Danny nodded. 'My sister Ruth and her stressed-out husband, Kenny. They drove down from Reno yesterday in their rusty old Winnebago. As far as I understand, they both like to pray for healing. Ruth said she'd head up there first thing this morning to give the old man a blessing, so it's maybe best I'm not there.'

'You not the praying type, Officer Clark?' Leighton asked with a playful smile.

'No, I'm not. I guess I never really took to any kind of faith. I reckon you're either religious or you're not. Maybe it's hard-wired somewhere in the DNA.'

'That sounds about right.' Leighton said quietly. He had lost what little faith he had a decade earlier.

Danny frowned for a moment, clearly trying to give words to something perplexing. 'But sometimes, you know when we get a serious call to respond to something bad – a shooter maybe, or a fatality out on the highway – I think about it.'

'Think about what?' Leighton asked.

'The big stuff: where we came from; where we go after all this.'

'You mean, you think about it when you're scared?' Leighton asked with a sideways smile.

'Yeah, I guess. Do you ever think about your mortality, Jonesy?'

'Nope,' Leighton shrugged dismissively. 'The way I see it, fretting about the hereafter would be like spending summer worrying about winter. It may be coming, and it may be dark, but wasting your lovely warm days thinking about it would just be dumb. Plus, sometimes you get a sunny day, even in the middle of winter.'

'Very true, Master Yoda.'

Leighton grinned and pressed his hands together and bowed his head in a momentary gesture of ancient wisdom.

Both officers watched as a couple of rubber-clad windsurfers carried their gear down the slipway and slid out onto the rippling water. Leighton kept his eyes fixed on the ocean for a moment, formulating his words, then half turned to face his partner.

'Listen, Danny, I was thinking that maybe I could cover for you,' Leighton said, trying to make it sound easy. 'You know, if you wanted to have a couple of hours up at the hospital with your old man each day? Maybe you could split the time with your sis, just to make it a bit easier on both of you.'

'You would do that?' Danny blew into the air and seemed to relax a little at the idea.

'Sure,' Leighton shrugged. 'We're only down for morning watch this week. Even today we only have highway monitoring and a Driver Safety class – I reckon I can handle that. C'mon, let's get going. I'll drop you at the hospital and you can work it out from there.'

'You're a good guy, Jonesy,' Danny said with a relieved smile.

'Yeah?' Leighton frowned. 'Maybe someone could try telling that to my teenage daughter.'

2

At 10 a.m. the sun was already hot over Oceanside, but there was enough of a fresh breeze coming in off the sea to keep things comfortable. Dave Rollins was using a canary-yellow cloth to polish the dashboard of a 1992 Duster – thinking about how he could correct his deteriorating golf game – when he noticed the woman. Like most used car salesmen, Rollins, who had been running this game for thirty years, seemed to have a sixth sense that informed him when potential customers had entered the car lot. There was no fence around the place, only a large square area of fluttering red and green metallic flags. Yet, even though it was a plain old lot, it still managed to attract plenty of buyers. In the past six months Rollins had shifted more than seventy cars, all of which had brought the prospect of retiring to perfect his golf game that bit closer. All he needed to make a sale was the combination of a used car and a customer.

This time, the person of interest was over on the north side of the lot, which bordered the groaning freeway. When Rollins caught a glimpse of her moving between the cars, he gave the gearstick a quick polish then stuffed the duster into his trouser pocket.

After spraying a mist of peppermint freshener into his mouth, Rollins glanced in the rear-view mirror, smoothed down his greying hair, and leapt out of the refreshed vehicle.

Snaking his way between several parked cars, he checked his reflection in a number of gleaming windows. At fifty-two years of age, the decades of Californian sun had carved deep lines into his bronze skin, but Dave felt that gave him an air of maturity and wisdom.

'Hey there, darling,' he called out as he approached the woman. 'Beautiful morning, isn't it?'

The woman, however, did not respond to his greeting. Instead, she stood defiantly with her hands on her hips.

'Where did this car come from?' She pointed accusatively to an innocuous silver Ford, which was parked inside the boundary of the lot.

'Excuse me?' Rollins was momentarily knocked off balance. This was usually his territory to rule over, and customers did not usually hit him with questions unless they pertained to paint finishes or mileage.

'This car,' the woman said, in slow syllables as if speaking to a child. 'Who owns it? Why is it even here?' As she spoke, she peered suspiciously at the vehicle, as if she were expecting it to bite her.

'What?' Rollins laughed. By that time, based on her garish attire, he'd realised the woman in front of him was a hooker. Most likely she was high on something too – they often were. 'This is a car lot,' he said dismissively, 'what did you expect to find here, Flamingos?'

'Whose car is it?' The woman repeated her question, undaunted by the man's attempt to assert his limited authority.

Rollins glanced at the vehicle. He didn't recognise it as being one of his own, but he wasn't about to start discussing that fact with some ten-dollar hooker – especially when some real customers could show up at any moment.

'Look,' he said with a grimace, 'just get out of here, sweetheart, before I call the cops.'

'I'm not going anywhere until you answer my question!' the woman said.

'Well,' Rollins took a deep breath and inflated his chest. 'I guess I'll just have to drag you out of the place myself.'

At that moment, the woman eyed him from head to toe and laughed at the prospect. He was a short man with a pot belly and manicured nails; the woman had faced down larger threats than him.

'You try to touch me, and you'll regret it,' Rochelle said in a matter-of-fact manner.

Something in the cool watchfulness of the woman's eyes caused Dave Rollins to momentarily consider his position. If he had been a wiser man, he would simply have walked away muttering to himself. However, his fragile sense of masculinity had to be defended.

'The hell I will, bitch!' he sneered.

As Dave Rollins lunged toward the woman, she quickly dipped her hand into her cheap handbag and produced a small can of Mace. Before the raging salesman could shift his trajectory, the woman deftly sprayed the stinging substance directly into his face. He stumbled away from her, toward his office trailer, holding his face like a bad actor in a late-night horror movie.

The woman shrugged in a gesture of quiet indifference. She had to deal with dangerous men every other day.

'I did warn you,' she said dismissively, before returning her attention to the car.

3

After he'd returned from discretely disposing of the leftovers in the dry grass at the edge of Carpenter Road, the man showered, put on a towel robe, and made his way along a narrow corridor to the rear of the house. He felt satisfied and excited. The other killing – the first one – had been different. It had come from anger and a need for revenge. But tonight, the experience had been different. It had been purer.

The building was a relatively modern home, and it stood in a small, private garden on the eastern part of the city. This was an area characterised by miles of neat, secure homes, existing in entrenched isolation from each other. A four-foot-tall, peach coloured wall hemmed in the garden, and provided much-needed shade from the scorching afternoon sun. The building comprised of a living area and two bedrooms; however, the one at the rear of the property was the important one. That was the memory room. The space was not particularly big, but it featured two large windows, which provided wonderful views across the Southern Californian valley. If you looked south, you could catch a glimpse of the Pacific Ocean. But the view was not the reason he had chosen this part of the house as his refuge: it was because it offered him the best quality light for his project.

In terms of layout, the room was a simple square shape and painted white. It contained only a few items of furniture: a small wooden desk, a plastic, office chair and a waste paper bin. The walls were blank, except for one that was split horizontally by a long wooden shelf, upon which sat a small, tattered jewellery box. An expensive ring from two decades earlier rested in the box, along with a more precious item from the same summer in 1987.

Moving toward the shelf, like a holy man reaching out to some profound relic, he brought his hand up close to where the small box sat. He was careful not to let his hand touch it, because then he would have to open the box and entire days might be lost to his labyrinth of memories. Instead, he gently placed a new memento on the shelf and took a step back to look at it.

The small red tin of lip gloss was circular and featured a garish cartoon of two cherries. The previous evening, he had momentarily considered leaving it behind, on that dusty dead-end street, when he'd disposed of the remains, but he'd held on to it – as well as his other small trophy. During the trip, the body was sitting upright in the backseat of the car, held in place by a seatbelt, appearing to the naïve world to be a sleeping passenger. This had been much easier than placing it in the trunk, which was fine when his captive was alive, whimpering and praying, but not when he had finished with them. He had discovered on previous occasions that rigor mortis would set in soon after death, and a previously soft body would set hard like marble, locking the body into shape. Steel-like limbs, set hard at strange angles, made it difficult to remove the remains from the trunk. However, with his upright corpse, Michael could simply unclip the seatbelt, pull the body over, and let it tumble easily from the car.

He had removed the faux fur jacket from the body to make applying the seatbelt easier, but, as he pulled the body from the car, the red tin of lip gloss had rolled like a small wheel from the folds of the garment. Having deposited the remains amongst some dried grasses on the edge of Carpenter Road, he returned to the vehicle and picked up the small red tin. He was about to launch it through the air, into the arid undergrowth, but something had stopped him. Perhaps the item reminded him of youthfulness, or the softness of a girl's mouth; whatever it was, a strange flicker of association had made him stuff it in his pocket before driving off to dump the car somewhere far away from the sprawled remains.

4

Leighton had only just pulled the police car out of the circular drop-off area of Tri City Medical Centre, when the crackling call came through from dispatch on his radio. He had been enjoying the view – the sky above the gleaming, white towers of the hospital was a flawless blue. This was Leighton's favourite time of year, when the Santa Ana winds would blow any smog out over the ocean, and, for a while at least, the city felt fresh and clean. The air had always seemed to smell like that, years earlier, on the days he had taken his young daughter, Annie, to the beach next to Tyson Street Park. It was their weekend ritual. She had loved the jungle gym there best of all. But that was before Annie had grown up, and Leighton's ability to parent had suddenly faltered. In recent months, he'd felt like his job was the only part of his life in which he had any clear sense of purpose – and that was wavering.

Leighton's nostalgic recollections were broken by the message coming through his radio:

'All units in the Harbour area – we have a report of an alleged assault on a car salesman by a female assailant. Incident is possibly in progress. Address is a commercial business: Rollins Stock Cars, 118 Connor Street.'

As he picked up the black handset, Leighton turned to his imaginary partner and nodded, as if in confirmation.

'Ten-four dispatch,' he said, 'this is Leighton Jones, me and Danny are in the area. We will take it – en route.'

Leighton knew from experience that a minor incident like this would probably involve nothing more than an unhappy customer getting revenge for being sold a pile of junk. Therefore, the situation was unlikely to escalate to the point of requiring backup officers to arrive at the scene and ask tricky questions regarding the whereabouts of Officer Daniel Clark.

Less than five minutes after he received the call from dispatch, Leighton pulled up outside the Rollins Stock car lot. He switched off the engine and reached for the radio to call in his position.

'Dispatch, this is Car B33 at location on West Visa Way.'

As he stepped out of the vehicle, Leighton felt the warm air on his skin and heard the distant sound of the ocean waves – it was a calming, reassuring sound. Mixed with this was the jagged sound of raised voices. The antagonism was loud enough to be heard over the rushing sounds of the freeway, as well as the distant thunder of the ocean. Pausing for a moment, Leighton sighed and dragged a hand over his face. The argument reminded him a bit too much of home.

Making his way through the maze of gleaming vehicles, Leighton followed the swelling sound until he finally located its source.

When he arrived in the centre of the car lot, Leighton found a young woman standing defiantly in front of a clearly enraged man, on the driver's side of a silver Ford. More alarming was the fact that the woman was holding a small can of pepper spray. The scene reminded Leighton of old vampire movies, in which a monster could be held back by a glowing crucifix or tiny vial of holy water. An area of red skin on the man's right cheek, coupled with a watering, bloodshot eye, suggested to Leighton that the woman had already given the can a spray or two.

'Okay, ma'am,' Leighton called out to the woman. 'I'm a police officer, put the Mace down.'

She glanced briefly toward Leighton, dismissed him and returned her entire attention to the red-faced male.

'I said, put the Mace down,' Leighton spoke again – this time in a deliberately calm and clear manner.

'Not as long as that prick is within grabbing distance of me.'

Leighton nodded to the man. 'Take a step back, sir. Please.'

Dave Rollins shook his head in irritation but obeyed the police officer's instruction.

'Okay, Miss …' Leighton gestured to the hand holding the Mace. The woman gradually lowered it but kept it in her hand.

'That's good. Now can somebody tell me what's going on here?'

'That crazy bitch just tried to blind me with that pepper spray,' Rollins shouted.

'Is that true?' Leighton asked, as he glanced at the young woman.

'He tried to grab me,' she shrugged, 'I was defending myself.'

'She was trespassing!' Rollins whined.

'Sir, do you work here?' Leighton asked.

'Of course, I do. My name is David Rollins – as in Rollins Stock Cars. I've been here for sixteen years. I own all of this.' Even in this moment of chaos, he couldn't resist the opportunity to bathe in pride.

Leighton nodded his head and shifted his attention to the woman.

'What's your name, Miss?' he asked.

She shrugged and brushed at nothing on her shoulder.

'I need a name,' Leighton continued.

'Rochelle,' she said quickly.

'Okay, thank you.' Leighton took a slow and deliberate breath. 'Now, what are you doing in this used car lot, Rochelle?'

'I was walking along the street out there,' she pointed to the highway, 'when I spotted this car. Some bitch climbed into it two nights ago, along with my jacket and my phone.'

'That's obviously bullshit, she's high on something,' Rollins shouted.

Rochelle narrowed her eyes and flicked her middle finger at the salesman.

'Sir,' Leighton said, 'you're really not helping.'

Leighton walked slowly to the rear of the car, crouched down, and made a note of the license plate.

'Do you own this vehicle?' he asked Rollins.

'No, it's not one of mine. The ones I sell all have blank plates.'

'Yeah, I noticed that. I thought it might be your own private car, but it's not?' Leighton asked.

'Of course it's not,' Rollins said, with a frown like a knife cut between his eyes. 'Do you think I'd drive that piece of shit?'

Leighton ignored the question. 'Tell me, do those fancy cameras you have mounted on poles all around here actually record anything?'

'Of course, we have twenty-four-hour surveillance.'

'Where's the recording equipment?'

'Back in my office. It runs on a 48-hour loop.'

'Mr Rollins, could you please go and check that a recording was made last night?'

When Dave Rollins had skulked away, Leighton's demeanour softened, and he turned to Rochelle.

'Okay, let's make a deal. How about you take a walk, I appease Mr Rollins, and we all get to go our separate ways in time for lunch.'

'That's my jacket in there,' Rochelle said defiantly, and folded her arms. 'I'm not leaving without it.'

'Okay, ma'am, if it is, could you explain how your jacket got inside this car?'

'I told you already, I gave it to some girl last night, over on the South Cal Freeway, but the bitch made off with it.'

'Was she working the streets too?'

'Oh no, this girl was a regular princess, smoking outside some café place down by the lighthouse.'

Leighton nodded, a non-committal expression on his face, and looked through the window at the raggedy faux fur jacket, raising his eyebrows.

Rochelle followed his gaze and felt the need to explain. 'Look, I know, it's a shitty jacket, but I think she was probably more interested in the forty bucks in the inside pocket.'

Leighton sighed and walked over to the driver's side door and tried the handle.

'It's locked, Sherlock,' Rochelle said, with one hand on her hip. 'Don't you think I would have tried the door already?'

'All of them?' Leighton asked, as he moved purposefully around the car.

'No but I fig—'

There was an audible click as Leighton opened the rear door. He reached into the Ford and cautiously pulled out the worn garment. He would normally have checked the pockets, but he didn't want to risk a needle-stick from a hooker's jacket, so he was happy to let this one slide.

'Okay,' he said, as he handed Rochelle the jacket, 'seems like you've got what you wanted.'

But Rochelle wasn't listening: she was frantically checking her pockets.

'Looks like the bitch got my cherry lip gloss, but at least the cash is here. You want to make a poster or something, telling people to watch out for a coat-stealing bitch with a flame tattoo on her scrawny little neck.'

She pulled out a thin roll of notes and counted them, her lips moving silently in time with her fingers. 'All here,' she said with a satisfied smile.

'Look,' Leighton said quietly, 'if I were you, I'd clear out of here pretty quickly. That guy could insist that I charge you with assault.'

'You're not taking me in?' she said, sounding genuinely surprised.

'Nope,' Leighton said dismissively.

'What, not even for the power trip?'

'No power trip required.'

'Are you sure you're a real cop?' she asked.

'Sometimes I ask myself the same thing,' Leighton said with a wry smile, but Rochelle had already turned around and was moving through an aisle of cars.

At that moment, Leighton heard Rollins returning from his office. He turned to greet and divert him. 'Any luck?' he asked.

'There was nothing recorded last night, camera must've been acting up. Where the hell's she going?' Rollins asked.

Leighton was unsure if Dave Rollins was the kind of petty man who would demand that he drop the full weight of the law upon a poor girl who clearly had enough problems to deal with. He suspected that he was.

Therefore, he said the one thing that he knew would get Rollins off the subject.

'Hey,' Leighton said, whilst rubbing his neck thoughtfully, 'I was thinking about getting a run-around for my daughter. She's seventeen and almost ready to sit her driver's test. Do you have anything like that?'

'I sure do!' Dave Rollins said with a wide grin.

5

After he had left Dave Rollins' car lot, Leighton spent three hours in a meeting room at the back of the station, delivering a Driver Awareness class to a group of seven people. Each of them had been involved in a minor traffic collision or had been caught DUI. Even with the windows open and the ceiling fan on, the afternoon session had been long and hot. Leighton had felt increasingly tired as he'd explained the difference between thinking distance, stopping distance and breaking distance. Eventually he wrapped up the theory and led the party of offenders outside where they had each been required to lay out coloured cones to mark out what they estimated the stopping distance of a car being driven at 60mph to be. Each person had placed a separate cone to show their guess. As was always the case, all of their guesses were vastly underestimated. When they were all finished, Leighton took a mangled licence plate from a cardboard box that was on the concrete steps of the meeting room entrance. He then asked the group to pay close attention as he walked across the parking lot. Once he had covered the distance of seventeen cars, he placed the plate down on the ground.

'This,' he called back to the assembled group, 'is how far your car would travel after you had decided to stop.' He then waved the unsettled party over to where he was standing. Once they had all joined him, Leighton pointed to the ground.

'Okay, ladies and gentlemen, the licence plate at my feet came from a car that belonged to Mr Larry Spacey. Anyone heard of him?'

The various offenders shook their heads.

'I didn't think so.' Leighton continued. 'Larry was a local resident who killed two children over on Haymar Drive. The two brothers were aged eight and ten at the time. Anyway, on Thursday, 7 November, last year, the boys had sneaked across the road to get some party balloons from Dollar Tree for their three-year-old sister's birthday.' Leighton waited a moment to let the gravity of the situation sink in.

'It had been a dry afternoon, but as the boys made their way back home it had started to rain, and I guess that meant they had to hurry. They must have figured that Larry's saloon was travelling at the usual speed for that road – 40 mph. He wasn't. Our investigation concluded that Larry was driving at 68 mph. When he looked through that rain-soaked windshield, and saw the young boys run out in front of his car, he slammed his feet on the brake. The boys must have heard the squeal of Larry's tyres and froze. After the car had ploughed into the two boys, it continued to travel for another ten car lengths. Larry Spacey is currently serving a sentence of twenty-six years in jail. But, I got to see his eyes in the courtroom, and I can say confidently that his sentence will never end.' Leighton sighed, and picked up the mangled metal plate. 'Drive safely, and drive soberly, ladies and gentlemen. That concludes the Driver Awareness session, please ensure you collect any personal belongings, and sign out at reception.'

When he had finally cleared up the plastic cones from the parking bays, Leighton climbed into the Explorer and drove back across the city to the hospital to pick up Danny. Arriving at the vast parking area he found his partner, standing in the visitor drop-off zone, looking weary.

'Hey,' Leighton said, as Danny climbed into the car, 'how's your pop holding up?'

Danny rubbed one of his eyes. 'I don't know. They're not sure of anything. Apparently, he needs another MRI scan to confirm the scale of the damage.'

'Well, maybe that's a good thing,' Leighton said optimistically. 'At least you will know what's going on, right?'

'I hope so, Jonesy, I really do,' Danny said with a sigh. 'How was your day?'

'Pretty uneventful – just the way I like it,' Leighton said, and steered the car out of the hospital grounds. He wasn't being evasive – at that point, the incident at Rollins Stock Cars was still fairly insignificant; as far as he was concerned, the allegedly stolen jacket had been dealt with.

The two officers sped down the baking highway in the black and white Explorer. Leighton had deliberately chosen to visit anywhere that other Oceanside PD colleagues would be likely to see Danny in the vehicle.

For a while they parked in an observation point to watch the traffic on the Boulevard.

Finally, at the end of watch, Leighton dropped Danny at his small apartment on the east side of Mission Avenue, three streets away from the station.

'Thanks for today, Jonesy,' he said earnestly.

'Forget it, I can cover the shifts easily enough. Just keep your cell phone switched on in case I need to steal you away from the hospital.'

'You want me to write up some notes with you? We could head over to the station.'

Leighton shook his head. 'I'll take care of it. That way I can put in accurate details of when and where things happened.'

'Well, how about Friday night I buy you dinner? There's that fancy place you like down at the harbour?'

'That sounds nice, Danny, but the way I see it, you need to save your cash to pay your old man's medical bills. How about you buy me a beer sometime?'

'Sure,' Danny said, as he climbed out of the car, 'a crateful.'

As he pulled into the drive of his own small condo, Leighton sighed. A row of empty grey bins stood along the roadside like a guard of honour. The previous evening, Leighton had deliberately reminded his daughter to put out the trash for collection, but his own overflowing trash can remained by the side of the house. It seemed that Annie had forgotten again. This was nothing new. In recent months, Leighton had found that parenting his teenage daughter on his own was about as easy as putting handcuffs on a snake. He regularly found himself veering between being too soft, and overly critical.

When he stepped into his home, Leighton found Annie sitting on the sofa, eating a pretzel, and flicking through a glossy magazine.

'Hey,' she said, without shifting her attention from the images of moody, underweight models.

'Hi honey,' Leighton said whilst walking into the kitchen, 'how's your day been?'

'Good,' Annie said, shrugging her shoulders.

'You forgot to put out the trash can again.' Leighton poured himself a glass of water from the refrigerator and returned to the living area.

Annie frowned. 'Isn't it Wednesday that the garbage gets picked up?'

'Nope,' Leighton said resolutely, walking back into the room, 'it's always Monday, Annie.'

'Oops,' his daughter shrugged, and briskly turned another page in her magazine.

Leighton considered letting go of the fact that his daughter was still wearing her pyjamas at 6pm. but, as this had been the case for more than a month, it was too much to ignore.

'You decided not to get dressed again today?' he asked and took another sip from his glass.

'Why? I'm not going out anywhere,' she said, without looking up from the pages, 'and it's practically evening.'

Leighton looked at her for a moment and felt torn between love and concern. He knew she hated the way he always seemed to be lecturing her – he did too, it wasn't the type of dad he wanted to be, but he also knew how easily doing nothing can become normal, then consuming, and eventually depressing.

'School finished three months ago, honey. You need to find something to do.'

'I've actually been looking for work you know.' She tried to sound casual, but she began turning the pages with quick irritated flicks of her hand.

'So maybe you need to up your game? Step up to the plate? When the going gets tough and all that.'

'Hey, it's not like I'm living the party lifestyle here!' she said with a sullen frown.

'No?' Leighton's voice shifted to an angrier tone. 'So, who stayed over last night?'

'Nobody.'

'Don't lie to me, Annie,' Leighton sighed. 'There's two pizza boxes crushed in the trashcan outside.'

She shrugged. 'A friend came over last night, it was late, and I was afraid.'

'You were afraid?' Leighton raised his eyebrows. 'Was this a male friend?'

'Maybe,' Annie said, and looked straight ahead.

'Maybe is not an answer.'

'Yes, jeez!' Annie threw the magazine down on the floor. 'It was a male friend who stayed over. So, what?'

'So, in order to be safe, you let a stranger share your bed? Very wise.'

'I was afraid. I already told you. Sam is a guy I went to school with. He's nice.'

'Annie, your dad's a cop, there's an intruder alarm with motion sensors, and there's a Taser in each nightstand. I really don't think your *guest* was here to make you feel safe.'

'Nothing happened,' she said, her voice wavering.

'I didn't ask if it had,' Leighton said, 'but there's a poorly concealed hickey on your neck and a Trojan wrapper floating in the toilet, which suggest otherwise.'

'Jeez, do you ever switch out of *Robocop* dad mode?'

'Do you ever switch out of trashy daughter mode?'

There was a moment of silence in which Leighton wished he could retract his question.

'I'm seventeen,' she said defiantly, 'I can do what the hell I like.'

'Maybe in the outside world, or in your friend Lina's big old mansion, but not in my house whilst I'm paying for you to do "what the hell you like".' Leighton turned and walked toward the kitchen, but Annie wasn't quite finished.

'So, would you prefer I was living on the streets?' she called after him. Leighton stopped and turned around to look at her.

'No, baby,' Leighton said softly, 'I'd prefer you were making something of yourself – of achieving what I know you're capable of. Which is more than lying around all day watching TV and reading magazines.'

Annie stood up but avoided eye contact with her father.

'I'm going to Lina's place, so you don't need to worry about any *guests* tonight.'

'Oh, c'mon, I give you some basic house rules and you stomp off? You can't run away from your problems.'

'You did with mum.' Annie threw her words like a weapon. This was payback for his 'trashy daughter' comment.

For a moment there was silence, and both of them knew it was a cheap shot.

'That's not fair.' Leighton looked at the floor. 'Your mum's problems, her depression, couldn't be fixed – at least not by me.'

'Other people might have tried,' Annie said, but she only sounded half-convinced of her own claim.

'Well, I guess I'm not other people,' Leighton said quietly, 'you got me. Your mum's gone and I'm to blame. I'm sorry, Annie.' He turned and walked into the kitchen to wash his glass.

'So, you can't lecture me, you're no better,' Annie called after Leighton, but there was no need: his fight had gone.

Leighton walked back into the room and looked at his daughter. She was fiery and beautiful, and he wished that he could make her understand that he only wanted her to grow up happy and safe.

'Annie, you're right,' he said. 'I messed up. I married your mum and I didn't know what to do to help her. I tried different things, but I wasn't an expert, and, in the end, I failed. But maybe that's why you should listen to me. People who have messed up can help you avoid the mistakes they made.'

'Dad,' she looked at him with something close to pity, 'you don't learn from other people's mistakes, only your own. I'm still going to Lina's.'

'You don't need to go anywhere. I'm just taking a shower then I'm heading out, so you'll get some peace.'

'Where are you going?'

'Work,' Leighton said, with a casual shrug.

'But you just got back in from work. Haven't you given enough of your day to Oceanside PD?' Annie frowned and picked up her magazine.

'I know, honey,' Leighton shrugged, 'but I'm covering for a friend whose father is dying. I need to go and fill in some paperwork on his behalf or the captain will fire us both.'

'But you are coming back tonight, right?' Annie asked.

'Yeah, before dark, so we can talk then. I can bring some takeout?'

'Maybe,' Annie said, but while Leighton was in the shower, she sent a text to her friend Lina, asking to get picked up.

6

As her cheap pink plastic alarm started beeping, Rochelle rolled over in bed with a groan. One hand fluttered from beneath her crumpled sheets to hit the snooze button. The third time she heard the alarm, Rochelle slowly sat up. Her fold-down bed was in a crumbling two roomed apartment, in an almost entirely industrial part of the city. In this area, the air had none of the freshness of the nearby coast. The erratic air conditioner drew in the chemical vapour and stench of nearby businesses.

After clambering out of bed, standing up, and stretching until some bones in her lower back cracked, Rochelle stumbled bleary-eyed to the small kitchen area. She slumped down at the plastic picnic table and rummaged through the debris covering it. Eventually, she picked up a foil-wrapped burrito, ate half of it and threw the remainder into the trashcan.

She moved the microwave and used a steel knife to prise a loose tile off the wall. Reaching into the deep cavity behind it, Rochelle removed a large bag of white powder and a thick brown envelope – both of which she carried to the cluttered kitchen table. She sat down and yawned, and without realising, she licked her lips.

She picked up the envelope and carefully slid out its contents. The worn property brochure featured details of homes for sale in Wisconsin. The homes were two thousand miles from Oceanside, but, to Rochelle, the distance seemed further than that. She may as well have been looking at properties for sale in Narnia.

As she opened the property brochure, Rochelle felt a deep ache that had little to do with her physical state. She had gazed at the images so often each day that she knew each of them better than the building she had lived in for four years; yet she still took her time as her red plastic nails carefully traced each image.

After closing the brochure and sliding it carefully back in the envelope, Rochelle sighed and shifted her attention to the plastic bag. She slid the zip lock open and used the knife to extract a small mound of cocaine from the bag before holding it up to her face and inhaling it through her nose. The rushing euphoria was just enough to mask her deeper craving for a different life.

She shook her head, as if to clear water from her ears, and returned the envelope and the bag to the hole in the wall. Only after this ritual was complete was she ready to get showered and go to work.

7

It was after 8pm but still a warm evening when Leighton arrived back at work. Having parked his red Duster amongst the glossy black and whites of Oceanside station, he walked in through the locker room and passed a number of pinboards featuring a range of notices. He stopped outside the dispatch room where a small red-haired woman was typing at a computer, whilst a second woman spoke into a microphone.

'Hey, Lisa,' Leighton said in a hushed voice, 'how you are doing this evening?'

'Hi, Jonesy,' she said with a warm smile. 'I'm good. I thought you were on day shift?'

'Yeah, I was, I just need to catch up on some paperwork. It's like being in the third grade all over again. How are things in mission command, quiet I hope?'

'Pretty quiet so far – thankfully – a break-in up on the Heights, a stolen car, and a ten-fifty-four just called in an hour ago.'

'What was the location of the last one?' Leighton asked.

Lisa peered at the screen for a moment. 'It was pretty far out. Yeah, out at the edge of Carpenter Road. Some kids out on their bikes found a body lying in the grass at the side of the road.'

'Not good, sounds like Homicide's bag,' Leighton said, with a small shake of his head. 'Any details on the victim?'

'Nope,' Lisa shrugged. 'Jane Doe so far, but you know how quickly things can change around here.'

'Well, everything except for the decor.'

'Never a truer word! You want me to keep you posted?'

'It's okay, thanks,' Leighton said with a smile. 'I'm simply a traffic man.'

'Don't put yourself down, Jonesy. You've got a nose for this stuff. Some of the guys working in operations here wouldn't recognise a criminal if they were wearing a ski mask and a T-shirt that said, "Bad Guy". You're smarter than that … most of the time,' she said with a wink.

'Thanks,' he said. 'I think.'

'Is there any word on Danny's old man?' the second woman asked whilst now typing into her own computer.

'Still just the same, Maria. The doctors are running some tests apparently. But I'll let him know you guys were asking after him. He'll appreciate it.'

Leighton turned to go but Lisa held up her hand to halt him and cocked her head as she listened intently to her headset. She began to type rapidly as she spoke.

'Hang on, Jonesy, there are some details coming through on your Jane Doe: confirmed as dead, height five two, estimated to be twenty to thirty years of age, brunette, no distinguishing marks other than a tattoo on her neck,' she shrugged, 'no personal items found at the scene.'

Leighton, who had almost turned away, twisted around. 'Can you repeat that last part?'

'No personal items?' Lisa asked.

'Before that, something about a tattoo?'

'Sure,' Lisa checked the screen. 'Hang on, one of the techies is still adding the data. Yep, the recovered body has a tattoo on the neck. The system doesn't include a description yet. That mean something to you?'

'No, probably not. Thanks, ladies,' Leighton said, and left the room.

He moved out of the dispatch area and entered the corridor leading to the office area that was shared by General Crime and Traffic Division. As he passed by a colleague, Charlie Cox, who worked in another Traffic unit on most of the evening shifts, Leighton nodded a greeting.

'Hey, Charlie, have a safe one out there tonight.'

'Thanks Jonesy, I'll do my best. Listen, you should keep your head down buddy – Gretsch is looking for you,' the smaller man said, with an expression that suggested the captain was looking for trouble. That would be nothing new. At the age of forty-nine, Leighton was more experienced and much less malleable than many of the newer recruits. This was an endless source of irritation for the youngest of the station's four captains, who wanted to stamp his authority on everyone beneath him as he clambered his way the top.

'Thanks for the heads-up, Charlie,' Leighton said with a wink, and made his way carefully to his small booth at the back of the office.

Leighton sat down at his neat work station and rubbed his tired eyes. Sleep, which had eluded him for his first two decades on the force, seemed harder to escape as he approached fifty. If he remained in one position for too long, he would feel his eyes droop. He needed some chemical assistance to perk him up.

After grabbing a much-needed coffee from one of the two filter machines in the office, Leighton returned to his seat and tapped his login details into the computer. While the system went through the laborious process of signing him in, Leighton glanced at the only photograph on his cramped desk. It was a small picture of Annie as a kid. The girl in the frame was smiling and hugging a stuffed toy bird. Leighton responded to the small smile with one of his own. He could remember the exact day the photograph had been taken. Annie had been so pleased with the gift that she had fastened herself around her dad's neck and refused to stop hugging him for ten minutes. Afterwards, she had insisted that he take a picture of her holding the new pet. He remembered that they had made banana pancakes with maple syrup for supper that night, and they'd curled up together on the couch to watch silly cartoons. Annie had laughed so much that Leighton had worried she might eject the earlier supper. Those were golden times, but, like most of the precious things in Leighton's life, he hadn't appreciated them until they were gone.

After using two fingers to laboriously type up his record of the day's duties – describing the actions taken by himself and (allegedly) Officer Clark – Leighton sighed and leaned back in his creaking chair. The image of a girl in a borrowed jacket, standing at the back of the Beach House Café, flickered in his mind. He reflected on the hooker's claim about the girl who had stolen her garment. In Leighton's mind, something was wrong about the whole thing. It didn't make sense that a customer from a restaurant would steal a prostitute's grubby jacket, and run off with it into the deep, dark night. However, it seemed even less likely that the thief would leave a rolled-up bundle of ten dollar bills behind, along with the jacket. Still, whatever holes were shot through the story, it wasn't his problem to solve. Even if the Jane Doe turned out to be the girl from the corner, the guys in Homicide could easily put the pieces together.

Leighton yawned, and rubbed his tired eyes in an attempt to move his mind on to something else; yet the persistent thought wouldn't go away. He kept imagining how, under different circumstances, it could have been his daughter standing on the corner that night. God only knew he saw little enough of her – she could be out wandering along the same streets as every psycho in Oceanside. What if Annie and Lina had been in that café? His daughter could just as easily have stepped outside for some fresh air and vanished. The terror linked to that image motivated Leighton to gather more information.

Leaning forwards to the computer, Leighton's fingers clicked on the keyboard and brought up a list of current incidents. He found the details of the recovered body on Carpenter Road and clicked the print icon. A few moments later, a machine at the other side of the office began to shudder. Leighton shut down his machine and stood up. Having made his way across the room, he grabbed the warm pages from the plastic tray beneath the printer. It wouldn't do any harm to have a look. Nothing more.

8

An unseen Boeing 747 roared overhead, defying gravity as it rumbled into the night sky. The area at the rear of the Airways parking lot was too far away from the glowing cubicle of the security office to be visible. It was a vast area of anonymous cars, located beneath intermittent lights on the northern edge of Oceanside Municipal Airport. The illuminated rectangle of the terminal building was visible in the distance.

Even though there were several sodium lights mounted on tall poles around the area, there were, thankfully, no security cameras. That was one of the main reasons he had chosen to take a vehicle from this specific location. There were many, busier parking lots dotted all over Oceanside, but almost all were either too busy – making it likely that he would be interrupted – or they had some type of surveillance system. This place did have a couple of cameras, but they were both mounted at the yellow entrance and exit barriers, half a mile from the shadowy corner he was concealed in. However, a far more important reason for selecting a car from this location, was that the Airways lot was a long stay facility. Therefore, the cars parked in this area were unlikely to be reported missing for at least a few days. That gave him time to use the vehicle, dump the remains, and get home to clean himself up. By that time the trail would be cold; natural decomposition and the elements would help to conceal his crime. The airport parking lot had another significant benefit: he needed to take the car from somewhere that held many different vehicles as the chances of finding a left-hand drive car, parked on the street, would be slim.

As he slid the slim bar of flexible steel between the glass and the car door, the man was lost in the past, thinking about how

Veronica should have been the one. If it had worked out, back in 1988, everything would have been different. In a way it was partly her fault, but he couldn't blame her entirely. It was clear to him that fate never played fair. You would only ever have what you wanted in life for a moment. Everything was transitory. This meant spending half your life wishing for something, and the other half wishing it away. In that sense, Veronica's death had given him something magical – a dark purpose – to create something permanent.

He leaned against the car window and pulled the slim bar upwards; he felt it hook under the door mechanism. With a practised ease, he shifted his pressure and felt the resistance of the lock disappear. The car door opened, and he slid inside.

Yet, even whilst committing the crime, he still he tried to convince himself that in another life, he wouldn't have had to do any of this: he wouldn't have to break into vehicles; he wouldn't have to keep looking for other girls who looked like her; he wouldn't have to keep killing them.

As he used a flat screwdriver to access the car's ignition mechanism, he considered how part of him – the part still vaguely connected to the real world – liked to pretend that it would stop eventually. In reality, it was unlikely.

He pulled two wires out of the steel key chamber and touched them together. There was a momentary spark and the engine rumbled into life.

'It's alive,' he said with a grim smile. He put the car into gear and drove out of the airport, onto the freeway leading into the city.

9

The darkening sky overhead was fading from soft orange at one end, into bruised purple, and finally black at the other. Leighton, who had been driving around the harbour area, slowed the car to a stop, and looked across the road to where a woman was pacing the corner, between a drive-through liquor store and a body shop, in demented circles. Leighton slid down the window of his car and leaned out.

'Excuse me, miss,' he called.

The woman turned at the sound of his voice and hurried over to Leighton's car. The length of her heels made the short journey difficult and her clicking heels sounded like tiny teeth biting the sidewalk.

'I'm looking for a girl named Rochelle,' he said, 'I think she works this area too.'

'Hey there handsome.' The woman looked older close up, and when she smiled she revealed a missing incisor. 'I can be Rochelle, Michelle – whoever you want me to be.'

'It's okay,' Leighton held up a hand and smiled, 'it has to be this one in particular. I just need to speak to her.'

'That's what they all say, honey.'

'Have you seen her?' he asked hopefully.

'Rochelle, all leopard-print and pretty eyes, sure, I've seen her.' The girl turned away, focusing on a car that was passing slowly on the other side of the street.

'Where was this?' Leighton continued.

'Huh?' she glanced back, irritated.

'Where did you see her?'

'Time is money, honey,' she said, and held out an expectant hand.

Leighton opened his jacket and revealed the gold badge pinned to the inside.

'You asshole!' the woman spat on the ground. 'I might have guessed.'

'Where is she?' Leighton repeated.

'I don't know who you're talking about, never seen her before.'

'C'mon,' Leighton said softly, 'this is off the record. She's not in trouble, I just need to speak to her. Please. I think someone she knows got hurt.'

Eventually the woman sighed and shook her head. 'She's over on Seagaze Drive, at least she was half an hour ago. Hope the bitch is worth it.'

'Thanks,' Leighton said, and handed her a twenty-dollar bill before driving off.

He had been cruising the area in wide, looping circles for almost ten minutes before he finally recognised a familiar figure, pacing back and forth on the sidewalk, on the opposite side of the street to him. The woman looked more confident than she had when he'd encountered her in the car lot, but this was, of course, her territory. After pulling the car over, Leighton called across the street to her.

'Hey there, Rochelle, isn't it?' he shouted from the car window. 'Can we talk?'

The young woman glanced across the street for a moment then turned around and walked deliberately in the opposite direction.

'Shit.' Leighton made a U-turn and pulled up alongside her.

This time, he leaned out of the window as he drew level with her.

'Hey you're Rochelle, right? Remember me – Officer Jones? I just need to speak to you.'

'Get lost, you're bad for business. If I'm seen speaking to you, every Joe in the street will think I'm undercover.' Rochelle began to walk away but Leighton drove the car slowly alongside her.

'Please, just get in,' Leighton said. 'We can go for a coffee somewhere. Or a beer.'

Rochelle stopped walking and glanced at him suspiciously before she sighed, 'Jeez, okay. But just for a beer, no freebies.'

'Nothing else, I promise,' Leighton said disarmingly.

Rochelle looked in disgust at the back seat where some papers were scattered.

'So, do I get to sit up front?'

'Why not,' Leighton shrugged, 'I guess I've already broken enough rules today.'

'Where's your partner?' Rochelle asked as she climbed into the car. 'I thought you guys always travelled in pairs.'

'I guess I'm not that popular,' Leighton smiled. 'And anyway, I'm off duty.'

The Red Rooster was a dive bar favoured by cops – active and retired. Inside, it was a plain affair with a tired wooden interior, and a scuffed pool table to one side of the seating area. Leighton and Rochelle selected a table in a dimly-lit back corner and sat down. Rochelle gazed at the multi-coloured football flags that were stuck above the bar. A jukebox was playing some Springsteen songs, just loud enough to keep the toes of the regulars tapping along.

'So, is this where you cops come to watch the big game then?'

'Only when we are off duty,' Leighton said with a smile.

'Yeah, sure.' Rochelle nodded her head but appeared unconvinced.

'Give me a second,' Leighton said, as he got up from the table.

'You hungry?' he asked, as he returned from the bar and placed two cold bottles of beer on the table.

'Yeah, but I'm watching my figure. Doesn't help to carry any weight in my line of work.'

'Yeah, not in mine either – slows you down. Cheers.' Leighton clinked the neck of his bottle against Rochelle's and took a sip of beer. As she sipped her own, Rochelle frowned at him. 'Hey, should a traffic cop really be cruising around DUI?'

Leighton smiled and carefully turned around his bottle to expose the label.

'Coors – low alcohol,' he said with a smile, 'all the taste and none of the fatalities.'

Rochelle eyes widened as she quickly checked her own label and was visibly relieved to see it was a regular beer.

'Thank God! I didn't want you feeding me some fake beer,' she said, and took another gulp as if to test it. 'So, what is it you want to know?' she asked, as she absently used a long fingernail to tear at the gold foil on the neck of her bottle.

'The night you met the girl – the one who took your jacket – which evening was it?'

Rochelle shrugged. 'Thursday, or Friday maybe.'

'Which one?' Leighton said softly, 'I need you to be sure.'

'Friday, yeah, definitely Friday.'

'How can you be sure?' Leighton asked.

'Well, the Texan guy I'd been with that afternoon was in town for the football game on Saturday. He kept saying that he wished he could see me the next day, but with the game and all …'

'You reckoned the girl you spoke to was outside a bar?'

'Not a bar, a café – that place with all the surfboards on the walls, down at the harbour. You know it?'

'Yeah, I think so,' Leighton said.

'Did you find the bitch?'

'Yes. Well, maybe.' Leighton held Rochelle's gaze. 'It's possible the girl didn't rob you. I just want to check it out.'

'But what makes you think she didn't?' Rochelle frowned, clearly reluctant to let go of her resentment.

'A body turned up this morning. It's early days, but they said she had a tattoo on the side of her neck. I just reckon it might match your description of the girl.'

'Shit,' Rochelle shook her head and turned away from Leighton. 'When you say dead, what you mean is …?'

'As in, no longer alive.'

'I know that, wise ass. Dead is dead. Do you mean she was hit by a car, or had an OD?'

'No.'

'So, what *are* you saying? That she was killed?'

'We don't know. Possibly.'

Rochelle said nothing. Instead, she took a large gulp of beer from the bottle, and deliberately looked around, trying unsuccessfully to appear unaffected. Eventually, after a few minutes, she brought her gaze back to Leighton.

'How come you're interested in this shit?' she asked. 'Shouldn't it be your buddies in the murder division, or whatever it's called, chasing it up? I thought you guys in Traffic were more into catching speeding assholes?'

'I guess I'm just interested. I know it's not my case, so, you're right, Homicide will probably follow it up.'

'Whatever,' Rochelle yawned. 'Hey, do you think she was killed because someone mistook her for a hooker? I mean, she was wearing my jacket, standing on the street, you know?'

'It's possible,' Leighton shrugged. 'It's not even my case, like you say, I just thought that after meeting you, maybe there was something I could help figure out.'

'Yeah, well I'm sure that hookers get killed every goddamned week in California, so good luck figuring it out.'

'Look, do you mind taking a drive down there with me?'

'Where?'

'To the café at the harbour.'

'Sure, if I get something to eat there, right?'

'Right,' Leighton said with a wry smile. 'I thought you weren't hungry?'

'Not for shitty bar food. I could do with some of that healthy beachside cuisine – an omelette maybe.'

'Okay,' Leighton laughed, 'we'll take a drive down, but finish your beer, there's no rush.'

As they left the Rooster, Leighton returned the empty bottles to the bar, where an elderly barman with a small beard was wiping down the beer taps with a cloth. He nodded to Leighton and smiled.

'Thanks, Jonesy, you trying to steal my job?'

'Just trying to save your old legs,' Leighton said with a wink. 'See you Friday, Rikki.'

'Sure thing,' the older man replied.

Another man, who was hunched at the opposite end of the bar, turned on his stool and watched Leighton and Rochelle leave. He frowned and stared at the door long after they had left.

'Something bothering you, son?' the barman asked.

'What?' the man said absently. 'Oh, no, I just thought I recognised that guy.'

10

Some foods fill you up, others leave you wanting more. When he been a child, that was how he had responded to candy. He could vaguely recall getting a box of Hershey bars, from some faceless relative, as a Christmas gift. Despite a stern warning not to eat them all at once, he'd found the temptation too great. He had gorged himself, and yet the urge to have more continued inside him.

Now, in the darkness of the present day, it was like that with his late-night drives, and all those girls, looking just like her, selling their bodies on the streets. There was such a plentiful supply right in front of him. It was almost as if the world wanted him to get rid of them.

He parked the stolen car in a shadowy side road, just off Seagate Way, and savoured the moment. This was always his favourite part: no past memories and no fear of getting caught. Instead there was the all-consuming thrill. He was dressed in dark clothes and was almost invisible. From this position, he could easily observe the girl he had chosen – a lone figure, working on a nearby corner. She would appear beneath the streetlight then vanish in a truck or a car, only to reappear a short time later. Although she would perk up when a passing car slowed down, most of the time she leaned back against the streetlight looking tired. That was good. It meant she would be less likely to put up a struggle.

Sometimes the girl would be gone for a little longer, and he would worry that, in his hubris, he had waited too long, and she had decided to head home for the night. But she always came back – returning to the streetlight like a moth to a flame.

As the hours ticked by, he felt no need to rush. He would simply enjoy watching her and wondering about the inside of her mouth.

11

Having parked his car on the street outside the Beach House Café, Leighton unclipped his seatbelt and turned to face Rochelle.

'Now this place looks a bit nicer than the Rooster, so don't go looking for business around the tables,' Leighton said with a smile.

'Screw you!' Rochelle said, appearing to be genuinely angry.

'Hey,' Leighton held up his hands to placate her. 'Relax, I was only joking.'

'So was I,' Rochelle said with a wink. 'And anyway, I've still got to make a living.' She reached into her pocket and produced a lipstick, which she promptly applied before she and Leighton got out of the car.

The café was a typical hacienda-style building with cream coloured walls, and rust coloured tiles on the roof. However, as they stepped into the warm night and approached the café, Leighton and Rochelle discovered that the place was closed for the evening.

'What the hell?' Rochelle peered through the glass much as she had several nights earlier, only this time the inside was dark and deserted.

Leighton was a small distance away, peering at an illuminated menu that was mounted in a gold frame next to the locked front door. 'Says here that the place closes at 6.30pm. midweek, and 10pm. Friday and Saturday.'

'So much for an omelette.' Rochelle said, and took a packet of cigarettes out of her bag. As she lit one, she glanced around for potential customers then remembered she was standing next to a cop. 'Are we done here?' she asked, clearly restless. 'I have to earn some rent money, you know.'

Leighton walked over to her from the door of the café.

'Yeah, almost done,' he said quietly, and looked at Rochelle. 'Is this definitely the place?'

'Yes,' Rochelle sighed, 'it is *definitely* the place.'

'Okay, can you point to the last place you saw the girl? Where exactly was she standing?'

'Well, we were both standing smoking *exactly* here. Then we swapped jackets and—'

Leighton looked at her quizzically. 'Why would she want your jacket if she had one of her own?'

'She didn't make like she wanted to keep the jacket. I needed to use the bathroom, so she gave me hers – so I wouldn't be recognised as the scum of the earth by the saintly customers.'

'Ah, I get it,' Leighton nodded. 'So, she was still standing out here when you went inside?'

Rochelle nodded. 'That's what I said.'

'Then what?'

'I did my thing in the bathroom and came back out here. That's when I found she'd vanished, along with my stuff.' Rochelle shrugged. 'She got into her car, or whatever.'

'You said that you saw the car. Where was it, out here on the freeway?'

'No,' Rochelle sighed impatiently, 'come on, I'll show you. But then I'm done with this bullshit.' She strode ahead to the corner of the sand coloured building, leaving Leighton to hurry after her. She led him round the back of the café to the parking lot and showed him where she had stood the previous Friday night.

'I'd only just got to about here,' she pointed at the ground, 'when the car almost knocked me down as it raced out of here. I guess she was inside it.'

'Because you found the jacket?' Leighton asked.

Rochelle nodded. 'Yeah, but I found my lighter too – the one I had given her. It was lying over there,' she said, and pointed to the empty parking bay where the silver saloon had sat.

Leighton wandered over to the place Rochelle had pointed out. Crouching down for a moment he peered around and bit his bottom lip. Then he stood up, smiled, and looked back toward the young woman.

'Rochelle, you've been very helpful, thanks for doing this.' Leighton walked back over to her. 'Can I drop you back home?'

'Hell, no, I'm good right here.'

'Do you really think you're safe down here – especially given recent events?'

Rochelle turned around and looked at him as if he had suggested that she went skipping home to her pink princess castle.

'I'm a hooker, Officer,' she said, and shrugged her shoulders. 'There is nowhere safe for us.'

With her unarguable point made, Rochelle turned and walked off into the night, her high heels clicking on the sidewalk. Leighton was left with a strange sense of concern for a woman who was probably emotionally stronger than he was. He dismissed his self-indulgence and walked across the parking lot to stand where Rochelle said she had seen the car. Crouching down again, he scanned the ground, unsure of what he was looking for. He glanced momentarily upwards and spotted the gas station across the freeway. The shop area was at the wrong angle for anyone inside to have seen this parking area. However, even at this distance, Leighton could see that the station did have a number of CCTV cameras mounted around the forecourt.

Crossing the highway was a risky business during the day, and it was even more dangerous at night. Leighton waited for a large enough gap to open before he ran across all four lanes. A large truck acknowledged his stupidity with a throaty blast of its horns.

On the other side, Leighton crossed the coldly lit forecourt of the gas station and entered the brightly lit shop. The place was filled with automobile spares, magazines, and cut-price cartons of beer. At the far end of the shop, a young man was serving the only other customer. Leighton allowed the elderly man in the yellow shirt to finish his transaction, approached the counter, and held up his badge.

'Oceanside PD.'

The young guy in the checked shirt who was serving looked horrified, and he began to lick his bottom lip nervously.

'Is this about those kids with the six packs?' he volunteered. 'Godammit, I knew as soon as they'd left. I saw them high-five each other, out there on the court, I'm telling you the honest truth, Officer, I swear I thought their ID was genuine.'

'Take it easy, son.' Leighton spoke slowly to help calm the mood. 'I only want to ask about your security cameras.'

'Oh Jeez, sorry. It's just I had these college kids in here buying Wild Turkey and beer. They looked kinda young, but they had ID and it looked, you know, authentic.'

Looking at the kid behind the counter, Leighton estimated that he couldn't be much older than the college kids sneaking around for beers. It was more than likely that this kid had simply been supplying some friends with beer without too many questions. In any case, Leighton had more pressing concerns, so he gave the kid the benefit of the doubt.

'Appearances can be deceptive,' Leighton said. 'Now, do those security cameras out on the forecourt work?'

'Yeah, sure,' the young guy nodded. 'Well, three out of the four are good; the one above the door fogs up a little, but they do all work.'

'What do you record the footage on, video tapes?'

'Yeah, one for each shift, there are fourteen in all. The boss keeps promising to get us one of those hard drive recorders, but I reckon he likes to keep us all busy.'

'What day is changeover day for the tapes?'

'Wednesday.'

'So, you still have the tape from Friday night?'

'Yeah sure – number ten. Give me a second.'

Leighton gazed absently at the items for sale, while the young man rummaged around frantically in a drawer behind the counter. Eventually he popped up, grinning like a pearl diver coming up for air.

'Here you go,' he said, and held out a plastic video cassette tape.

'Do you mind if I take this?' Leighton asked.

'Sure,' the clerk shrugged, 'we have plenty of spares – those tapes are cheap shit.'

'Should match my VCR pretty well.'

'You still got one of those things at home?' the young man asked.

'Yeah,' Leighton shrugged, 'I'm old school all the way.'

'Wow!' The young man seemed both horrified and impressed.

'Thanks kid,' Leighton said as he left the shop.

The young man let out a relieved sigh, sounding like a swimmer who had stayed underwater for too long.

12

Although she was not the most observant young woman, Jenna Dodds instinctively knew that something was wrong when the car had pulled up on the dark street ahead of her. It had been a slow night, with nothing more than a handjob for a trucker in his cab, and a nervous college guy who couldn't get it up in the back of his Kia so had sheepishly asked for his money back. Luckily, he had been too embarrassed to make a fuss, and Jenna had given him half of his forty dollars back.

After that she had wandered away from Highway 76, along Benet Road, and on to the quieter Via Del Monte. This was a vast landscape of industrial units, which was usually lifeless after dark; however, in these deserted spaces there were also fewer customers. The whole area was a flat expanse of cracked parking lots, low buildings, and the occasional palm tree. Sometimes she would get picked up by a delivery driver making the most of the remote location and a willing participant.

In a funny way, she liked walking in this area rather than in the bustle of downtown – there was less competition and it was quieter. As she wandered next to the buildings, Jenna would sometimes imagine that she worked inside some of them. She would gaze at the occasional illuminated window and pretend that she had a regular job, like mopping floors, instead of one involving some sweating man squeezing her face and neck whilst thrusting angrily at her body. If things had been different in high school, maybe she could have ended up having a different kind of life. But Darnel had got her pregnant when she was fifteen. After social services took the baby away, she didn't care so much about anything. It was a quick slide into alcohol, drugs, and then prostitution in exchange for crack. Then, after a short time, prostitution became as much of a habit as the crack.

Jenna was wandering past a long row of dark single-storey offices, when she heard the low groan of a car engine behind her. She half turned around and had to hold up an arm to shield her eyes against the fierce lights, whilst supressing her natural urge to shout some obscenities at the vehicle in case the driver was a potential client. Instead, she placed a hand on her hip and pushed out one leg as she watched the car go by.

Stopping to lean against an oversized sign that was advertising office space, Jenna felt a fresh sense of optimism as the car slowed down, and finally stopped.

Once it had paused at the kerbside, the vehicle lurched forward crazily a couple of times, and then the engine died.

In that moment, Jenna decided optimistically that the car was being driven by a potential customer. She promptly applied some peach coloured lipstick and strutted toward the red brake lights.

However, before she reached the car, a door was flung open. The driver, dressed in a dark tracksuit, jumped out and glanced nervously both ways before running off into the night.

Jenna, who had spent all of her twenty-three years living in a trailer park, was used to seeing 'jacked' cars being hastily abandoned. Sometimes, they were bait cars; other times the stolen vehicle had run out of gas, miles from the jacker's home, leaving them stranded in enemy territory. She had even heard that some, more modern cars, could be shut down remotely, but this old saloon car didn't look fancy enough for that type of technology, so she concluded that it had simply ran out of juice.

'Shit!' Jenna kicked at the sidewalk and then turned around. A bad night was only getting worse. She suspected that she might have better luck down by the highway – where there were more cars. Of course, there was also a greater chance of getting busted by the cops, but it was evolving into a slow night and she had no other option. If she returned home with anything less than sixty bucks, Darnel would smack her around and send her back out again, and she knew from bitter experience that it was even harder to attract customers with an eye swollen shut and a burst lip.

Jenna had only taken a couple of steps away from the lifeless car when she first heard the noise. The sound was initially unclear – it might have been nothing more than the ghostly echo of a radio that had been left playing, or perhaps the sound of a TV, wafting from an open window of a nearby office. But, when Jenna cocked her head and listened properly, she realised the sound was that of a woman crying. The voice was begging for help.

For a moment, Jenna thought about walking away – back toward the freeway. In this neighbourhood, it was often the smartest thing to do when you encountered a crime. However, she also knew that girls like herself were easy prey for any psycho with a grudge. For once in her life, Jenna could choose to do the right thing.

She desperately glanced around in the hope that somebody else might show up to help, but that entire section of Via Del Monte was mostly a mixture of industrial units and offices, which meant the place was a graveyard at night. This was what made it a good place to turn tricks without offending the law-abiding citizens of Oceanside.

The voice whimpered again. Jenna shuddered and stepped tentatively toward the car. As she approached the vehicle, the sound seemed much clearer and increasingly desperate.

She hunched over and took only tiny steps, giving her the appearance of someone approaching a bomb.

'Hello?' she called out toward the colourless car.

The voice suddenly fell silent, as if gauging whether or not Jenna was a threat. Then, suddenly, it began calling out again, with renewed desperation. The increase in volume allowed Jenna to pinpoint exactly where the sound was coming from. It was located deep within the trunk.

Jenna took a deep breath, opened the trunk, and took an instinctive step away from it.

Inside was a small, portable CD player. After a moment of silence, the begging started again, it was coming from the CD player, causing Jenna to jump with fright.

It was then, in the confusion of the moment, that she felt a strong arm fasten around her neck, and the chemical-soaked rag that was pressed against her face sent her tumbling helplessly into darkness.

'Hello, Veronica,' a voice said.

***

Less than two hours later, in the room at the rear of the house on Thorn Road, he sat hunched over the small desk with the two adjustable magnifying glasses locked into position. He liked to revisit the killing in his mind as he worked on the trophy he had removed from the victim. This was his favourite part of the ritual. It had only been an hour since he ended her life, but already he was busy.

Once the remains were found and buried, or cremated, this fragment would be all that remained, and it would belong to him entirely – his possession. But right now, at this moment, it was at the point of transfiguration: when something mortal becomes immortal. It was as if he was granting her new life – a better life.

He paused to wipe his chin when he realised, with a degree of satisfaction, he was actually drooling.

13

It was after 11pm. when Leighton finally returned home. After glancing at the dark windows for any sign of life in the bungalow, he climbed out of the car and locked it. A chorus of crickets fell silent as he approached the door, which was lit by a single overhead bulb. He hoped to hell that Annie didn't have company – it wouldn't heal their relationship very much if she had to watch her daddy throw her boyfriend out on his skinny white ass.

To help reduce the risk of this, Leighton decided he would make as much noise as he could when he opened the door. That way, if Annie did have a 'visitor', she would have enough time to hustle him out of her bedroom window. However, his efforts were unnecessary. The alarm began bleeping as soon as he stepped into the hallway. Leighton deftly opened a small panel on the wall behind the door and punched in a number of digits. With the alarm deactivated, he locked the door and wandered into the open living area. When he switched on the light, he discovered that the place looked surprisingly tidier than it had earlier in the evening. The magazines had been cleared from the small coffee table, and in their place was a neat white envelope.

Leighton sat on the sofa with a sigh and picked up the envelope.

It was a telephone bill, but a handwritten message had been scrawled across the back of it:

Gone to Lina's. A.x

He had sent her a text message half an hour earlier to ask if she wanted him to bring back some food, but she had not replied. The note explained why.

Leighton yawned and lay down on the couch. He looked carefully at the scrawled note. He could remember the nights he had spent, ten years earlier, sitting at the supper table helping Annie with her homework. He had always been amazed at how she would take so long practising her spelling, saying each letter slowly and clearly. Back then, he had stupidly thought her childhood would last for ever: that there would always be more time to spend with Annie. Part of him envisaged that he would somehow reach a later day, a better time, when he would be free to be the kind of dad he wanted to be – a good one.

He closed his eyes for a moment and felt himself begin to tumble backwards into oblivion. It took all of his strength to make himself sit up. He knew it would be a mistake to allow himself to fall asleep on the sofa – he would only regret it in the morning when he woke up crumpled, cold, and stiff.

After he'd dragged himself up from the sofa, Leighton stripped off and stepped into a hot shower. At one year away from his fifth decade, he was still a fit man, but his muscles were tight like coiled springs. Twenty years of workplace stress, combined with grief and insomnia, had left Leighton Jones unable to ever fully relax. A tall glass of rum would create an artificial sense of calm, but it was like covering a steel chair with a soft blanket. Thankfully, the torrents of hot water in the shower went some way to soothing his weary bones.

Leighton stepped, dripping, from the shower, and dried himself with a clean towel before slipping on a pair of grey boxer shorts and a white vest, then padded into the kitchen and returned with a glass that clinked with ice cubes and white rum.

Crossing the bedroom, he placed his glass next to the bed and sat on the edge of the mattress. The room around him was neat and clean: white walls and dark wooden furniture. All the surfaces were clear, with the exception of a small cassette player sitting on one of his bedside cabinets. The silence in the room didn't unsettle Leighton as much as it might other people. Sighing to himself, he leant forward and rubbed his hands over his face.

He'd become used to living without a wife – after the dream of 'happily ever after' had burst like a bubble, he had felt no real desire to create a new one; however, the absence of his daughter was a more palpable thing. They had been a solid unit for a long time. Before Gretsch had been appointed captain, his predecessor at the Mission Avenue station was a wise, old officer called Barney Feltzer. After Heather Jones had taken her own life in the bath of her elderly parents' home, everyone in the station was fairly sympathetic to Leighton's situation. The captain had quietly arranged for him to have permanent day shifts, therefore allowing him to spend evenings with his daughter. As she grew older, and spent the holidays at camp, Leighton worked three entire summers of nights to return the favour to his colleagues.

Around that time, he tried to ensure that Annie got involved in different activities-like swim class- in a naïve attempt to involve women in her life. He figured they might offer her the type of guidance Leighton never could- something like a mother's touch.

Mostly, however, it had been just the two of them. He would help Annie dress each morning, and then drop her at Mrs Carrera's – the childminder – before school. At the end of each shift he would return to pick her up. Often, she would be sitting at the kitchen table with a glass of milk and a plate of Oreo cookies, sketching some crazy picture of colourful birds or chunky rainbows. Annie would grin helplessly whenever she saw her father and her eyes would widen in joy. Now, in the silence of his empty home, those days felt like a different life entirely.

Here, in the silent apartment, Leighton felt the weight of his loss. He hoped, somehow, that the conflict of recent months would melt away, and that they could recapture the strong connection they had once shared.

Leighton lay back on his bed and closed his eyes. Perhaps, he thought, tomorrow would be a different day – a fresh start. It was then he remembered something that made him sit up and swing his legs to the floor: he had forgotten all about the video camera footage from the gas station.

Padding out of the bedroom, he made his way to the front door and unlocked it. The evening air was warm, and the crickets were chirruping throughout the garden as Leighton walked barefoot to his car. Somewhere in the darkness he could hear a garden sprinkler swishing to life.

When Leighton returned, he relocked the door and collected his drink from the bedroom. A moment later, he was sitting in the living area holding the video cassette in his hand. Crouching before his television, he slotted the cassette into the mouth of the VCR and pressed the play button. The image that appeared on the screen was a grainy shot of the gas station forecourt, with ghostly lights – from the headlights of passing cars – occasionally floating into view. After a moment Leighton's eyes adjusted to the view. It was an angular shot of the gas station that covered two of the pumps and switched jerkily every ten seconds to cover the other two. It was within the second shot that the parking lot of the Beach House Café could be seen, but only in the distance.

Leighton noted that the image of the lot wasn't too clear because the garage forecourt was so brightly lit. This meant that the distant parking lot had a misty quality, as if it were deep beneath some strange ocean. Leighton sipped his drink and pressed the fast-forward button on the remote control. He watched as cars appeared and vanished in an endless loop of activity. Combined with the black and white footage, the jumpiness of the scene reminded Leighton of the old Harold Lloyd movies he had watched as a kid.

After several minutes, Leighton leaned forward and peered at the screen. He used the remote control to pause the recording. A car had pulled into the car park, at the rear of the shot. The footage of the car was indistinct, and he was unable to identify the make or model, but the vehicle seemed to be parked in the bay that Rochelle had identified. 'Hello there,' he whispered.

Leighton released the pause button and watched transfixed as a figure climbed out of the car and vanished off to one side of the shot. The angle switched again – to the other gas pumps – leaving Leighton frowning in frustration as he forwarded the footage. Eventually the image switched back to the car park. The car was still in place and the driver was still missing, but this time a female figure was visible at the edge of the screen. Leighton paused the tape again and closed in until his face was inches from the television screen. At first Leighton thought he was looking at Rochelle – the build and hair looked similar – but the walk was different. The girl at the edge of the frame dropped something on the ground, probably a cigarette, and twisted her foot on it. She turned away from the car and started walking back to the café. Then, something made her stop. Leighton took a deep breath and rewound the footage a couple of seconds. He peered in fascination as the girl repeated the motion with her foot. This time he watched more carefully as she moved away and stopped. Whatever had grabbed her attention could not be seen in the video. She turned and walked toward the car. Her movements suggested cautiousness and she was walking in an almost dreamlike way. She went round the car to the rear of it, where she reached down and opened the trunk.

At that moment, the image on the screen was shattered by jagged white lines. The VCR hummed loudly and began to whine like an animal in pain.

'Shit!' Leighton knocked over the remains of his drink as he desperately pressed different buttons on the remote. When that had little effect, he threw it to one side and began randomly pressing buttons on the VCR. The stop button made no difference so, finally, Leighton held down the power switch until the machine died. When he powered it back up again, he held down the eject button and watched as the tape exited smoothly from the mouth of the player. It was only when he pulled the cassette out fully, that he discovered the countless black curls of twisted tape that were connecting it to the machine.

'Shit!' In a moment of panic, Leighton pulled on one end of the cheap tape, only to have it snap in his hand like a rubber band.

Leighton knew, even if he could somehow reconnect the tape, it would never count as evidence. Anything could have been spliced in or out of the original footage. After gathering up the mangled tape and the cassette, Leighton took it through to the kitchen and deposited it in the trashcan.

14

He needed another one: it was not a matter of choice, it was a simple fact. He simply *had* to kill again. That irrefutable fact soothed him. If his desire was a need, a compulsion, then there was no personal responsibility involved – not really. The first death would be considered a crime of passion. He could see that now; it might even be possible that a reasonable jury would see that too. A half-decent lawyer, and maybe a psychiatric assessment, was all that would be required. The circumstances were such that most people would feel the same: first love is a powerful force and enough to drive a person to kill.

So, he could quite easily be forgiven for that.

However, the others since then had been different – yet no less instinctive. For a while, after the first one, he had felt better: the world had seemed right. But as he lay in the darkness of his bed, with infinity stretching like a black sea in front of him, he felt the need to return to the streets.

At first the images in his mind had simply been of her – Veronica – laughing and smiling in some distant summer. Sometimes she would fill his mind so vividly, it seemed achingly impossible that she no longer existed. At such moments he would reach beneath his pillow and remove the small box. Turning it over in his hands he would try to resist opening it, but the pull was always too strong. Eventually he would open the box and look at the treasure within and the urge would approach, and consume him like a wave, pulling him into the chaos. That was when he would go out in his car to surprise another girl.

That meant, really, he was not responsible for his actions.

15

Oceanside Police Station was already bustling at 7.50am. In a narrow corridor, near the rear of the building, Leighton had picked up the keys to the black Explorer and was leaning on the vehicle bookings counter, signing out the car, when he became aware of a presence behind him. He turned around to meet the critical gaze of Captain Gretsch.

'Morning, sir,' Leighton said with a brief smile, 'you taking a car out for a spin?'

'No,' Gretsch said sternly, 'I was looking for you actually.'

'Me, why?' Leighton was genuinely surprised: the captain had only spoken to him a handful of times in five years.

'I just wanted a chat,' Gretsch said, but there was no friendliness in his voice.

'Something bothering you, sir?'

'Not me,' he said, 'I'm here to ask if everything is okay with you, Officer Jones.'

'Everything is fine,' Leighton shrugged, 'I guess.'

'You guess?' Gretsch blew out, making a whistling noise, and shook his head. 'You know, that sounds fairly vague to me.'

Leighton sensed that the captain was enjoying this game a little too much.

'Is there a specific point to this, sir?'

'Where were you yesterday evening?' Gretsch asked.

'Here in the city,' Leighton replied with a smile.

'Be more specific,' Gretsch frowned.

'In Oceanside, California, USA.'

'Don't fuck with me, Jones!'

'That's funny, Captain, because it kinda feels to me like it's the other way around here.'

'I simply asked you a question, Officer.'

'Is there something specific you want to discuss, Captain?'

'Were you drinking in a bar yesterday, with a known prostitute, before getting behind the wheel of a vehicle?'

'Oh, you've got somebody spying on your own colleagues now? That's great. How to build an effective team.'

'Answer the goddam question!'

Leighton shifted his mindset to defensive mode. 'Well, yes, your source is correct. I was in a bar, where I used my own time to interview a witness to a traffic incident. During that time, I consumed a bottle of non-alcoholic beer. This detail will be corroborated by Rikki Trejo, the member of staff who served me. I also know that the Red Rooster tills are itemised, therefore, if you feel the need to pursue the matter, before involving Internal Affairs, you could cross-reference the security camera footage of me arriving at the bar, with the till records, which will show the purchase of said beer.'

'Okay, wise-guy. What incident were you investigating?'

'Vehicle theft, in accordance with my role as an officer in Traffic Division. A stolen Ford saloon was found abandoned in a local car dealership over on Wisconsin Avenue. A witness at the scene informed me that they may have had information regarding the perpetrator.'

'And where was Officer Clark whilst this "interview" was taking place? Apparently, you were seen alone with some woman.'

'As I told you already, Captain, this interview took place in my own, personal time. Officer Clark had already completed his watch for the day. If you want to know how we spent our time prior to that, it involved two hours on patrol across the city, a Driver Awareness class in the afternoon, and an hour of traffic monitoring on the Boulevard. But all of this is written up in our notes from yesterday – you can check over them if you want?'

'I already did,' Gretsch said as he walked away. 'I just wanted to make sure they were accurate. Luckily for you, they matched up … this time.'

Having asserted himself, the captain was no longer interested in Leighton, who was shaking his head in disbelief. Danny was entering the booking room just as Gretsch was leaving, and he stepped aside to let the captain pass by.

'Morning, Sir,' he said to the departing captain – who ignored him.

Danny turned to Leighton and shrugged. 'What did Captain Happy want?'

'Just to feel like a powerful man,' Leighton said with a wink.

'Don't mess with him, Jonesy. You know he's hoping to take over from Chief Winston when he retires in October?'

'Yeah, I heard that too, but I wanted to be Superman for most of my childhood, doesn't mean I can leap off a building.'

'If Gretsch ever makes chief, maybe you will.'

'I'll worry about it when it happens. Let's get to work.'

Leighton and Danny were crossing the Oceanside Police staff parking lot when a car horn blared at them. Leighton held up his hand in the baking heat to shield his eyes from the bright sun. A man was waving from behind the windshield of a small red Toyota. Leighton recognised the person trying to get his attention as Ed West – a field evidence technician – and waved back.

The smaller man clambered out of the car and approached the two traffic officers. He nodded to Danny but directed his attention to the older of the two.

'Hey, Jonesy, did you request the pickup of a stolen car from the Rollins Stock Cars dealership over on Wisconsin Ave?'

'Guilty as charged,' Leighton said with a smile.

'Well, you got lucky; we got a hit on it last night when we ran the plates. It had been reported stolen, but only recently.'

'How recent?' Leighton asked.

'Apparently, the owner, a Mr Guezardo, only made the report in the early hours of the morning.'

'But we brought it in on Monday, so why the delay with the report?'

'Guezardo was on a skiing trip with his family, only flew back in from Vermont last night.'

'Nice work, Ed. Was the car stolen from the home address?'

'Nope, a car park at the airport. Nice discovery to come home to. Worst I've ever had was finding a flat tyre after flying back up from Florida. Spent longer waiting for the repair truck than I did on the actual flight.'

'I don't suppose anything came up on the system for this Mr Guezardo?'

Ed shook his head. 'No warrants or priors, cleaner than most. Teaches physical education over at Whitney High School.'

'You still got the car in the cage?'

'Yeah, the guy's meant to be collecting it on Friday morning. You want me to drop a copy of the report in your tray?'

'Sure, thanks, Ed.' Leighton nodded, 'I'd appreciate the update.'

'No worries,' he said with a smile, 'you two have a safe one.'

'What was that about?' Danny asked as they got into the Explorer.

'A stolen car,' Leighton said as he adjusted the rear-view mirror. 'It's possibly linked to a homicide.'

'Hit and run?'

'Homicide,' Leighton said, starting the engine and putting on his sunglasses.

'Murder? Wow,' Danny said with a chuckle. 'I leave you alone for a couple of shifts and this is what happens.'

Leighton laughed and shrugged his shoulders. 'What can I say? The devil makes work for idle hands.'

'Which team has got the case?' Danny asked.

'Slater and Goza.'

Danny looked at Leighton, his expression revealing genuine concern for his partner. Oceanside PD was a small community and that meant it was easy to tread on someone else's toes.

'Well, you better be careful not to end up pissing on Detective Slater's backyard, you know how territorial these guys in Homicide can be.'

'It's okay,' Leighton said, 'I'll pass anything I find on to our detective colleagues, and they can go figure what happened. I got a video tape that I thought might have helped, but it got messed up in my VCR last night.'

'The video player probably didn't recognise something that wasn't a Clint Eastwood movie.'

'Nothing wrong with a bit of the old Wild West,' Leighton said wistfully. 'Keeping the peace was a simpler job back then.'

'Yeah, but I think "keeping the peace" simply involved shooting any lawbreakers,' Danny said.

'True,' Leighton conceded, 'but it also meant less paperwork, my friend.'

'Okay, I'm sold.' Danny smiled, and then looked at Leighton in a more anxious way. 'You promise to pass anything you get on to the big boys?'

'I promise; anything I find goes straight to the mighty Detective Slater.'

'Good plan,' Danny said, feeling only partly relieved. It wouldn't be the first time Leighton had veered into investigative territory that had led him across departmental and judicial boundaries. 'Right then, let's get you across to the medical centre.'

16

He liked the drive around the city most of all, when he had yet to choose the next one. That's what made it so special: tied to fate and the magic of the universe. He knew he would kill, but the victim was as unknown to him as he was to her.

Cruising beneath the tall palms and bright streetlights, he felt at the mercy of deeper and darker forces than the faceless people around him.

As he turned the steering wheel, and directed the vehicle through the streets of Oceanside, he held his grip loosely, as if he were dowsing for water in some sterile desert. It was a natural process: all he had to do was sit behind the windshield and relax; the car would find its way through the backstreets, truck stops and parking lots, to wherever the next Veronica would be waiting.

The greatest thrill of all – the climax of the drive – was when he spotted her. Most of the time she would be standing alone, in a bell jar of streetlight, and he would drive around the block, watching her, making sure, and all the while she would know nothing of her fate. The ordinary looking car, in which she would die only minutes later, could pass within feet of her three or four times, and she wouldn't even notice.

Tonight, he had acquired a navy saloon – from the airport as always. There had been a couple of left-hand drives parked fairly close to each other. This time he had got lucky with the one he'd chosen. When he opened the car, he discovered a spare key hidden behind an elastic band in the sun visor. That single development had saved him a few precious minutes, which meant he had more time to invest in finding, and playing with, his victim.

17

After dropping Danny at the hospital, Leighton drove out of the vast parking lot and cruised onto the highway. The traffic was already beginning to build up toward the relentless surge that would probably dominate the scorching roads until late afternoon. Having stopped momentarily to recover some abandoned road cones from the edge of the highway, and then to assist an angry businessman who was struggling to change a flat tire, Leighton eventually drove out to Carpenter Road: a wide grey road just off the San Luis Rey Mission Expressway. It cut through a number of used car parts dealers, but was mostly flanked by parched, scrubby land. Ultimately, the road led nowhere, and was therefore quiet during the day; it was mostly deserted at night. Leighton was fairly confident that whoever had come to dump a body here would have been able to do so without any real risk of being seen.

Leighton slowed his vehicle as he noticed the snapped remains of some crime scene ribbons fluttering in the light breeze at the side of the road. The moving scraps of plastic tape vaguely reminded him of the flags above the Rollins Stock Cars lot.

Pulling up on the opposite side of the road, Leighton climbed out of the Explorer. The car had powerful air conditioning and stepping away from it meant he was suddenly exposed to the intense heat of the bright morning. He put on a pair of sunglasses, moved to the back of the car, and opened the trunk. Everything in the rear of the vehicle was neatly arranged in different coloured, sturdy plastic crates. Each of the crates had a small label, taped on the side, naming the contents.

Leighton reached into the car, removed a plastic crate and carried it across the road toward the area of dry needle grass where the body had been found.

As he moved, Leighton felt the baking heat rising from the asphalt like a warm wave. He crossed the wide road and stepped carefully to the edge of the crime scene. After placing the crate down, he walked around, peering at the ground. Eventually he located a discernible patch where the colourless grass had been crushed by the weight of a body.

Returning to the crate, he removed a shallow plastic bowl, a bottle of water, and a plastic bag of white powder, which resembled the kind of stuff the Vice team brought into the station every other week. After pouring a mound of the white powder into the bowl, he unscrewed the lid of the water bottled and added a generous amount to the powder; he used a small trowel to stir the mixture until it began to thicken. He then poured some of the thick white paste on three different areas of the dusty ground, and spread each blob flat, as if smearing frosting on a birthday cake.

Once he had completed this process, Leighton returned the items to the crate and carried it back to the trunk of his car. He sat in the car and waited for ten minutes – with the door open to reduce the heat. Even with the fan running, it still felt too hot, but at least the plaster would set quickly. He reached across to his dashboard where a cassette tape was protruding. He pushed the tape in and closed his eyes as the sweet sound of blues music filled the air.

When he returned to the crime scene, he crouched down and tapped one of the plaster circles with his fingernail. It made a satisfying, dry clicking sound. He then reached into his shirt pocket and produced a small penknife, carefully unfolded the blade and used it to prise up the first of the three white discs. Turning it over in his hands, Leighton peered at the impression of the tyre. It was misshapen in places, where the ground had been too dry to allow a clear impression to form, but there were still a number of visible tread marks.

Once he had gathered up all three impressions, Leighton carried them, like misshaped dinner plates, to the trunk of his car where the soothing blues music was still playing. He placed each of the plaster casts alongside each other in the trunk and climbed into the driver's seat. Once the doors were closed, Leighton pressed a button on the dash to start the much-needed air conditioning. Leaning back in the seat, he reached into the side pocket of the car door, took out his cell phone and dialled his daughter's number.

'Hi, Annie, it's Dad.'

'Hi Dad,' she said in a husky voice, 'what's up?'

'Just checking in with you. You still at Lina's?'

'Yep,' she said with a long yawn, 'just about to have breakfast.'

'Sounds like you had a late night. You having something healthy?'

'Pop-Tarts.'

'Better than nothing,' Leighton said with a smile.

'Where are you, at the station?'

'Nope. I'm out making tire impressions from plaster in a dead-end street. I thought maybe I could hang a few around the house as a kind of modern art thing.'

'You're joking, right?' she giggled, but something in the tone of Annie's voice suggested she wasn't entirely sure.

'Yeah. Listen, Annie, I was thinking I could maybe take you to lunch?'

'That would be nice, Dad, but Lina wants to take a drive into town. I said I'd keep her company.'

'Lina, did she pass her test already?'

'Yeah, two weeks ago.'

'Well, after two weeks she's still just learning. Make sure she takes it easy.'

'She always does.'

'And wear your seatbelt.'

'I will.'

'You promise?'

'I promise.'

'Okay, honey, when will you be back? Tonight?'

'No, tomorrow, maybe, but I'll let you know.'

'You've got your key?'

'Sure.'

'Okay, I'll see you. I love you, kiddo.'

'Speak to you later, Dad,' she said, and hung up.

Leighton put down his phone and dragged two hands slowly down his face. His daughter was slipping further away from him every day and he didn't know how to fix it. The thought of her in a car with a newly qualified teenager at the wheel, on the chaos of the freeway, terrified him.

It was almost lunchtime when Leighton returned to the station. Thankfully, the silver car from the previous night was parked outside, along the back fence of the parking lot, with all the other seized vehicles. Having parked in a bay nearby, Leighton grabbed a couple of items and a sheet of white paper from the glovebox and made his way through the parking lot to the car. Looking at it in different circumstances, Leighton wondered if the victim's DNA would be all over the trunk, or the back seat, of the innocuous looking vehicle.

That type of evidence gathering was a fine art and would have to be authorised from above; collecting tire tracks might help justify a more detailed search – that was what he was hoping anyway, as he knelt beside the car. First, he checked to ensure that all the tyres were of the same type. They were all Marshalls – a fairly rare brand, which was good. Then, he opened a small ink pad and laid it on the ground, and took out a rubber roller, sliding it backwards and forwards over the pad until it was sufficiently coated. He took the roller to the near side tyre and rolled it over the curve of the tread from side to side. Finally, he took the paper and pressed it on the tyre. Running his hand over the sheet, he smoothed it down to ensure good contact. When he peeled the paper away from the tyre, it revealed a neat print of wavy blue lines. The image reminded Leighton of Annie's kindergarten paintings of the ocean.

After crossing the parking lot to the Explorer, Leighton opened the trunk and leaned in. He picked up one of the plaster casts from Carpenter Road and peered at it for a moment. He then looked at the printed paper in his other hand. They matched perfectly. Rochelle, it seemed, had been right – she had witnessed an abduction or possibly something worse than that.

18

Nina Shindel got a genuine fright when Leighton tapped her on the shoulder. She was listening to an audiobook through her headphones as she worked on removing a stubborn 9 mm bullet from the neck of a homicide victim. As an assistant medical examiner, she had no fear about handling the remains of the dead, but she hated the idea of people creeping up on her. Perhaps it was because, unlike most people, Nina got to see up close just how much damage humans could actually do to each other.

'Jeez,' she laughed, with relief as much as shock. She pulled off her earphones, leaving them dangling down the front of her lab coat. 'Can I help you?'

'Sorry for the scare, I'm Leighton Jones – I work Traffic. I don't know if you remember, but I think we spoke a little last year at the Police Department Christmas lunch.'

'We did?' Nina frowned as she pulled off a latex glove.

'Yeah,' Leighton grinned guiltily. 'I believe we were both avoiding the speeches. You're Nina, right?'

'Ah,' Nina smiled, 'I remember. You were the guy hiding out by the fountain.'

'Yeah, that was me. I'm not much of a fan of public speaking – from either side of the podium.'

'Don't worry,' she smiled, 'you're not alone there. So, what brings you down here?'

'I just wanted to ask you about the Jane Doe from Carpenter Road. Were you working on that case?'

'Sure,' Nina nodded, 'what exactly do you want to know?'

'Well, cause of death to start with,' Leighton said with a shrug.

'Asphyxiation. Most likely as a result of manual strangulation, by someone standing in front of her, looking her straight in the face.'

'Any foreign tissues present?' Leighton asked.

'Yeah, there was some evidence of sexual activity – non-penetrative. I found a couple of artificial fibres, but she had been left in the open, so they could simply be environmental. I still have to compare them with fibres recovered from the scene. They were passed on to your colleagues in Homicide. However, we lifted a partial print from her cheek. That might provide a quicker match. It's all in the report. Anyway, what's your interest? I didn't think Traffic were involved.'

'We're not. I'm just following up on a lead. Thanks for the update, I appreciate it.'

'There's more,' she said, 'but it'd probably be easier to show you.'

'Sure,' Leighton nodded.

Nina led him to the long row of square doors at the end of the room. She gripped a steel handle and pulled one of the doors open. Leighton instinctively took a step backwards as the pathologist removed the long tray that was holding the body. However, there was no need: unlike some of the human remains that Leighton had encountered throughout his career, this body had been cleaned – inside and out. Nina turned and looked at him as if he was a child.

'Get over here, officer. You're the one with the *interest* in the case.'

'You see this?' Nina indicated a plum coloured bruise on the neck and shoulder of the pale body.

'Where she was grabbed?'

'No, where she was strangled. Although she does have grab marks on her upper arms.'

Leighton peered at the porcelain skin of the cadaver's neck. Although the overhead fluorescent lighting had robbed the tattoo of any warmth, the three interlocking curves of flame were clearly visible.

'Nina, do you see many victims with tattoos?'

'Yeah, most of them – if the victim is under the age of fifty. And not all of them look like the artist had any training.'

'How many times have you seen a victim with this tattoo?'

Nina peered at it for a moment then glanced back at him.

'None that I can remember. Why?'

'A local prostitute may have spoken with a girl who vanished on Friday evening. I thought it may have been the victim, shortly before she was murdered. The prostitute said the girl she met had a flame tattoo on her neck.'

'Sounds possible. Where was she speaking to her?'

'Outside a café down at the harbour.'

'Well, this victim here had stomach contents amounting to fries and beer. If you can find out what the girl in the café ordered that night, I'd say you've got a pretty clear match. If you want to be really thorough, you could order the same meal from the café and bring it over here for me to compare the chemistry. But to be honest, the tattoo is unique.'

'Has anyone identified the body yet?' Leighton asked.

'No,' Nina said as she slid the tray back in, 'but she had no belongings on her, so it could take a few days.'

'Thanks, Nina, I appreciate you humouring me.'

'Any time, officer.'

'If I don't see you before, I'll see you at the next Christmas lunch.'

'Good plan, I'll meet you at the usual place, just as the speeches start.'

'Amen to that,' Leighton said, and left.

19

Leighton was sitting on the small wall outside the station. He had finished his shift half an hour earlier and was now enjoying the sensation of the warm sun on his face. He was feeling pretty pleased with himself, which was a unique experience for him. The information he had gathered on the case was good, and, if it led to an arrest, it might even get the captain off his back for a couple of weeks. The captain, who had been brought in to Oceanside PD to replace a warm and wise man, had never been particularly fond of Leighton, but perhaps that was because Leighton had never cared much for the captain. Gretsch represented the new breed of career police officers, who could use academic qualifications and initiatives to leapfrog their way to the top. This was exemplified by Gretsch's two degrees, which allowed people like him to avoid real police work, whilst sending others out on the streets.

Leighton stood up as Ryan Slater came out of the building. He was a tall, lean detective who looked like a coiled spring. Leighton had always felt that Slater had missed his true calling, in the United States Marine Corps.

'You got a minute?' Leighton asked.

'Sure,' Slater nodded, but kept walking briskly. 'What do you want?'

Leighton hurried alongside the younger man. 'This case involving the Jane Doe out on Carpenter Road, are you involved in the investigation?'

'Maybe, what about it?' Slater asked.

'I spoke to a witness who thinks your victim was abducted.'

'What witness?' Slater stopped walking and looked at Leighton with narrowed eyes.

'A working girl,' Leighton replied with a dismissive shrug of his shoulders. 'She was down at the harbour last Friday night.'

'A hooker? That's your witness? Jeez, Jonesy, I didn't realise you wanted to be a detective that badly,' Slater laughed in a humourless way.

'To be honest, Slater, I really don't want to spend my days dealing with death, but I met the witness during an alleged assault. She got me involved in this.'

'Was the assault on her?'

'*By* her, she was accused of attacking some used car salesman.'

'Okay, let me get this straight,' Slater said, holding out his spade hands as if estimating the size of an imaginary fish. 'When the cops show up to charge this violent hooker, she coincidentally puts herself forward as the star witness in murder case? Yeah, good luck taking that one to the DA.'

'It wasn't like that,' Leighton said flatly. 'She knows what she saw. She said the girl she spoke to had a flame tattoo on her neck, just like the victim's. That's more than a coincidence.'

'How the hell do you know about any tattoo on the victim?'

'I spoke to Nina Shindel.'

'Wow. You're crossing some serious boundaries, you do realise that?'

'Look, I may be a royal pain in the ass, but that doesn't change the facts – your victim was outside the Beach House Café.'

'Based on a hooker's claims and two people in California having the same tattoo?'

'There's a security tape with footage that corroborates her story.'

Slater stopped walking and ran a hand through his hair.

'Okay,' he said with a sigh, 'where exactly did you get this tape?'

'The gas station opposite the café where the girl was taken from.'

'So, where is this *tape* now?' Slater asked.

'It got destroyed.'

'Destroyed?' Slater rolled his eyes. 'Wow, a hooker in trouble makes up a story and the evidence gets destroyed – that's pretty convenient.'

'Look, don't be a dick, Slater. I got the tape, it was cheap, and it mangled in the machine before I got a chance to log it as evidence. But I have a set of tyre impressions that match the car that was probably used in the abduction and disposal of the body.'

'Where did you get tyre moulds from?'

'I made them myself out on Carpenter Road.'

'So, you've tampered with an active crime scene?' Slater's eyes widened.

'I took a drive out yesterday, after you guys had finished up there. The scene had been cleared by the technicians.'

As Leighton spoke, the detective looked at him with a mixture of disbelief and pity.

'Come on,' Leighton sighed. 'Why would I make this up?'

'I honestly don't know, but thankfully your oddball theories and missing evidence are all pretty academic now anyway.'

'Why is that?'

'We got a match on the DNA found on the victim. It belongs to some guy who works in the meatpacker over on Via De Monte – fifty yards from the scene. A car is going down to pick him up as we speak.'

'Well, maybe if you can tie him to the car, it would help make your case.'

'We've got DN-fucking-A – we don't need a couple of shitty tire prints and a mangled video tape.'

'So, what, the investigation is just over? You've got some DNA, so the case is closed, is it?'

'Not for me, but it is for you,' Slater said firmly, and walked away. 'When the Captain hears about this, you'll be up to your neck in a whole swamp of shit.'

'What's new?' Leighton whispered, and walked to his car. Given Slater's attitude, he was content to let the pieces of this investigation to fall whatever way they might. He had tried to pass on the details, which meant – regardless of how they were received – it was no longer his problem.

20

In the fifty years he had been sailing, Paul Milne was usually lucky when it came to fishing. Most mornings, before dawn, he would spend a couple of hours drifting along on the calm lake and return with at least four steelheads. In the past three decades, his wife had been rarely impressed by his catch. The only fish she was interested in eating came out of the icebox and had a crispy crumb coating. But her lack of enthusiasm made little difference to Paul, who was happy enough with the daily ritual, regardless of the catch. Today, however, was different.

He had been sitting in his small boat, on the mirror stillness of Lake Tanner, since 4.30am. without as much as a bite. Usually there would be two or three tugs on the line within the first hour, but it had been eerily quiet. To make matters worse, Paul's stainless-steel coffee flask was down to the last few bitter sips. However, it didn't really matter in the end; drifting in his small boat was where Paul found his peace and his rest. As a retired maths teacher, he had spent thirty hectic years being surrounded by thousands of young people with varying degrees of competency in numeracy. They would crush into his classroom and cram around his desk. By the time he retired, he'd felt like he was drowning in a sea of paperwork and marking and had a level of stress that prevented him from sleeping.

The teachers' lounge had offered little in the way of relaxation to Paul. He had therefore made the wise decision to retire at the age of fifty-eight. Yet the level of stress had not diminished, and Paul found himself plagued with months of restless anxiety. Eventually, having visited his physician, with twitching muscles and chronic insomnia, he was advised to spend more time amongst nature.

He had never been much of a hiker, and it seemed logical that he should engage with nature in the most familiar way, so Paul decided to spend every morning out on the water, far away from civilisation.

Paul was considering turning the boat around and heading back to shore when he first noticed the rock. Sometimes, if it had been a particularly dry year, the water level would fall, and larger boulders would gradually break the surface around the shoreline. To Paul, these newly exposed rocks resembled prehistoric eggs from an adventure movie. He could easily imagine one of them slowly cracking open as a pterodactyl broke its way out of its spherical home. But the rock that had appeared today was not at the shoreline: it was not even close to the edge. Instead, it was in the centre of the lake. It just didn't seem right.

Gripping the starter toggle for the small outboard motor, Paul pulled, and the engine roared to life. He crouched at the rear of the boat, guiding the neat little craft as it scored the surface of the lake. Within a few seconds he had arrived close to the rock. He cut the engine and let the boat drift toward it. The sudden shift in sound – from growling engine to absolute silence – was disconcerting, as if the natural world was holding its breath.

Finally, Paul arrived alongside the rock; it was then he discovered that it wasn't a rock. What Paul had initially mistaken for a sand coloured boulder, was in fact the sloped back of a naked body. It was floating, face down, in the lake, arms drifting outwards. The hair of the corpse spread out in the lapping water and moved with a lifelike motion, as if it were merely floating.

Paul, who had never seen death up close before – other than the occasional final gasps of a fish – felt his body shudder uncontrollably. His hands began to shake so dramatically that even when he locked his hands together, his forearms trembled, as if he were operating invisible machinery. The sensation lasted for several minutes, and when it had eventually subsided, he reached for the motor and started it again. He sped the small boat toward the shore, glad to be moving away from his grim discovery.

21

At 10.33 am., Leighton and Danny were sharing speed enforcement. Leighton was standing by their Explorer, at the side of the freeway, taking speed readings from the groaning traffic. In his right hand, he held a radar speed gun, which he frequently held up and pointed at passing vehicles. Most of the drivers would see the police officer and slow down. The more defiant ones would speed up, flicking a finger at the underpaid officer.

It was a particularly hot day, so Leighton and Danny were taking it in turns to sit in the car and listen out for any higher priorities – such as collisions.

When Danny approached Leighton, he was frowning.

'What's up, partner?' Leighton asked.

'I just heard a bunch of stuff about a body that was recovered out on Lake Tanner.'

'That's a fairly tricky place to get to. What are they calling it? Suicide?'

'Only if the victim strangled herself first, and then threw herself off Hudson point. They found one of her shoes and some drag marks up there next to the vantage point. I just thought it was maybe something linked to your jacket girl. Second female found in a week.'

'Well, it's not my concern anymore.' Leighton shrugged.

'Did you go and speak to Homicide, with what you've got on the case?'

'I tried to, but apparently Slater has the investigation all under control. Clearly doesn't want me contaminating his territory.'

'I can imagine,' Danny snorted, 'the guy's like a robot. Still, I didn't think it was in your nature to walk away from something like this.'

'What do you mean?' Leighton asked.

'C'mon. Every rookie in Oceanside has heard of that case you cracked at Pembleton with the Blanchette kid on the farm.'

'Oh, that,' Leighton sighed. 'I just got lucky there. There was no skill involved.'

'They say that everyone had given up on the case, but you kept going and found the girl, is that right?'

'Yeah,' Leighton kept his eye on the traffic. 'It was something like that, I don't really remember. All I know is that it damn near cost me my job.'

'So, what you gonna do this time?'

'Nothing,' Leighton said with a flicker of irritation. 'I told you, I'm staying away from the case.'

'I wish I could believe that,' Danny said, slowly shaking his head.

'You'll see,' Leighton replied, but he didn't sound too convinced himself.

22

It took almost fifteen minutes of pacing backwards and forwards, and smoking three cigarettes, before Rochelle finally summoned up enough courage to enter Oceanside Police Station. She had been hoping that Officer Leighton Jones would just walk out of the doors, or arrive whilst she was waiting. That way she could avoid setting foot inside the building. The last time she had been inside the place she was under arrest. Some surveillance operation – part of a crackdown on prostitution in Oceanside. Rochelle, along with six other young women, had been herded up and dragged into the station. No men, pimps or clients were charged, but the women were fingerprinted, searched and photographed by the proud arresting officers, as if the women were trophies from a big game hunt.

Eventually, realising that Officer Jones was not coming out anytime soon, Rochelle pushed through the large glass doors and stepped into the air-conditioned foyer.

Trying to hide her jitters, she crossed the tiled floor and shifted from foot to foot while she waited at the reception desk.

'Good afternoon,' the woman officer on reception said. 'How may I help you?'

'I need to speak to a guy who works here, I think his name is Officer Jones.'

'Can I ask what it's regarding?' the desk officer asked.

'Just some business,' Rochelle said, 'it's cool, he knows about it. We spoke already.'

'I'm afraid Officer Jones is out on duty at the moment.'

'Well can I, you know, leave a message for him?'

'Sure.' The officer grabbed a pen and a notepad and slid them both across the counter to Rochelle.

'You'll make sure Officer Jones gets it?' Rochelle called back.

'Yeah, relax, I will,' the officer said.

Luckily for Rochelle, she had already started to walk through the doors into the warm afternoon, when Captain Gretsch approached the reception area from a side door. He had only heard the last part of the conversation, but it was enough to pique his interest.

'Who was that?' Gretsch asked, his eyes fixed upon Rochelle as she walked toward the road outside.

'Some woman asking about Leighton Jones,' the officer said.

'What did she want you to write down?' Gretsch nodded to the A4 pad sitting in front of the officer.

'She just wanted to leave a message for him.'

'Tear out the page and throw it in the trash. The woman's clearly a hooker,' Gretsch said. 'She was never here. That idiot Jones is distracted enough from his job without this kind of shit.'

'Yes, sir.'

Gretsch waited to watch the officer rip the page from the pad and drop it in the wastepaper basket beneath the reception desk.

'Now, go to the bathroom and wash your goddam hands – use soap too – you don't know what, or who, she's touched.'

At the end of his shift, Leighton was standing in the back lot, using a serpentine yellow hose to wash down the Explorer, when he heard a female voice call to him from across the sea of police cars.

'Hey, Jonesy!'

He turned around to see a female officer waving to him from outside the glistening circle he was standing in.

'Hey, Denise,' he said with a warm smile, and he turned off the hose. The misty water vapour hung in the air making small rainbow arcs of colour.

'You looking to get your little Honda valeted? I can fit it in for a good price.'

'No, thanks,' she said with a grin, 'it's all clean – well, mostly. I just wanted to speak to you, if you've got a minute?'

'Sure,' Leighton said, as he stepped through the puddles to reach her, 'the turtle wax will keep till next time. Is everything okay?'

'Yeah, it's nothing bad. Just, well, a young woman stopped by earlier today. She was nervous as hell and hoping to speak to you.'

'Was it my daughter, Annie?' Leighton looked momentarily hopeful.

'No, I'd recognise your kid. This girl was older, possibly a working girl.'

'It's okay,' Leighton smiled and nodded, 'I know who you mean – all leopard-print and attitude, right?'

'That's the one. When I told her you were out, she asked to leave a message for you to call her.'

'Thanks, Denise. I appreciate you letting me know.'

'Not a problem,' Denise said, and turned to go, but she stopped.

'Look, Jonesy, it's maybe nothing, but the captain came up to the desk just after the girl left, he basically told me not to pass the message on to you.'

'Yeah, I can see how he might do that,' Leighton said, and shrugged his shoulders. 'I won't let it slip that you told me.'

'Thanks, Jonesy.'

'Now, you sure you don't need your jalopy washed?' Leighton asked hopefully and raised his eyebrows.

'I'm good,' Denise said, and she walked off as Leighton twisted the hose back on and continued to clean away the dirt and debris.

23

The following morning was hazy but warm; this meant that, down along the beach, the shifting ocean seemed to melt away into a horizon where sky and sea met. Three miles away, in South Ditmar Street, a barefoot Rochelle stepped out of one of the countless single-storey apartments that were crammed together in the Casa Bien development. A single road, Fenwick Avenue, ran in front of her home, connecting it to the busier road of Mission Avenue, but this was an area that few people chose to live in. The combination of low quality accommodation and relatively high crime made it an unattractive place in an otherwise attractive city.

Rochelle had a mane of tangled hair, and a smouldering cigarette was dangling from her lips. She was wearing a white vest and some grey sweatpants and was carrying a swollen garbage bag. As she approached her trashcan, Rochelle glanced up and was surprised to see Leighton across the street, leaning on his hood, reading a newspaper.

'Hey,' she called over to him with a partial smile on her lips.

'Good morning,' he said with a smile, and folded away the newspaper.

'How did you know where to find me?' Rochelle asked.

'I'm a cop,' Leighton said, and tapped his nose.

'Yeah, but you manage to hide it well.' Rochelle forcefully twisted the neck of her garbage bag and dropped it into the dented trashcan.

'I picked up a message at the station; it said you wanted to see me,' Leighton said.

'Yeah,' Rochelle said with a shrug, 'I wanted to speak to you about that missing girl, but not here. The locals around here can smell you guys from a mile away. They'd think I was a snitch. Give me a minute to grab some shoes. We can go someplace, okay?'

'Sure,' Leighton said, and got into the car.

When she reappeared, Rochelle was wearing a pair of white sneakers and had pulled her wild hair into a loose ponytail. She glanced around quickly before crossing the street and climbing into Leighton's car.

'So, where are we going?' he asked.

'Well, I figured that you still owe me an omelette,' Rochelle said as she fastened her seatbelt.

'Fair enough,' Leighton said with a wry smile. Judging by Rochelle's thin limbs, he figured she could do with a meal or two.

'Hey, but not at that freaky beach café place,' Rochelle said quickly, and then she seemed to check herself. 'If that's okay? I kinda feel like that place has an unlucky vibe to it.'

'It's okay,' Leighton said, 'I know a little place nearby that serves pretty good food.'

As Leighton drove toward the harbour, Rochelle gazed out of the car window, staring almost childlike at the prettier parts of the city.

'You okay there?' Leighton asked.

'It looks much better during the day – safer.'

'That's like most places,' Leighton said with a smile, 'except possibly Vegas.'

'Do you like it here?' Rochelle asked. 'Oceanside, I mean?'

'Yes, I think I do. You've got to remember; many people would love to live here.'

'I guess,' Rochelle said, and continued gazing out of the car window.

Oceanside's pier had stretched out over the waves, almost two thousand feet, since 1987. It was an unfussy construction of wood and steel. Leighton loved it: it was plain, sturdy and reliable. In an inexpressible way, he thought of it as somehow defiant, standing apart from the sturdier buildings of the rest of the city. At night, the pier looked like an illuminated sidewalk leading into the dark universe; during the day, it was home to a sprinkling of amiable fishermen – as well as the odd pelican.

At the far end of the pier was Ruby's - a retro-style diner, complete with a Wurlitzer jukebox and waitresses in red and white striped uniforms. It was here that Leighton was sitting opposite Rochelle at a small table, which was beside a long row of windows that looked out on the glimmering ocean below. Rochelle was eagerly devouring a ham omelette, whilst Leighton had opted for a tall mug of black coffee and some French toast.

Having spent the past decade interviewing witnesses of traffic accidents – sometimes involving fatalities – Leighton knew that people were less communicative when they were hungry. He was therefore content to let Rochelle eat before pushing her for any further information. Eventually, when they had both finished eating and were sipping their respective coffees, Leighton raised his eyebrows.

'So, pleasant as this is, what did you want to speak to me about?'

Rochelle leaned forward in her seat and spoke in a quiet, almost conspiratorial, voice.

'Well, I heard on the radio that they caught some guy for, you know, the murder of the girl with my jacket. Is that true?'

'What makes you think it's the same girl?' Leighton asked and took a sip of coffee.

'They said she had last vanished when out with colleagues at a local café. So, did they catch the guy or not?'

'Yeah,' Leighton nodded. 'That's what they're saying. But you seem to know as much as I do.'

'When did they get the guy?' Rochelle asked.

'Tuesday afternoon, as far as I know.'

'Do you know who he is?'

Leighton shook his head. 'Just some waste of space with a bunch of priors for rape and battery against women. But hey, he's locked up, so the streets are a little safer, right?'

'Maybe from your position but, I don't think so,' Rochelle said as she shook her head.

'What's that mean?'

'It means I don't think the streets are safer.'

'Why?'

'That's why I came to see you yesterday. I'm worried about a girl – Jenna – who works the Boulevard with me. She vanished on Wednesday night. I thought maybe the same sick bastard from last Friday had taken her, but if you said he was locked up on Tuesday then it couldn't have been him, right? So, there must be another asshole out there.'

'What do you mean, "she vanished"?' It was Leighton's turn to lean across the table.

Rochelle shrugged. 'Jenna is the kind of girl who will come out every night – even in the holidays – only for a couple of hours, but every single night. After last Wednesday, nobody seems to have seen her. A couple of girls have asked me about her, but she's just gone.'

'Couldn't she have spent the night with a client?'

'Not Jenna – she never stays out, ever. No motels either. She strictly does the front seats of cars or nothing.'

'Could she maybe be sick, taking a couple of nights off?' Leighton offered.

'I wondered about that too, but then her boyfriend Darnel has been driving around the usual corners looking for her. He's been asking all the girls if they've heard from her.'

'Look, I'd give it a few days,' Leighton said.

'You're right,' Rochelle said, and nodded. 'I guess I'm probably just spooked by the whole situation.'

'Well,' Leighton said sympathetically, 'it happens to us all at some point. Everybody gets unsettled by the scary stuff. But you've got to remember that these things are extremely rare. Hopefully the psycho who did this is locked up, and the rest of us can get back to normal.'

'I know,' Rochelle nodded again. 'It's just that I keep thinking about the resemblance thing.'

'What resemblance thing?' Leighton asked. He could feel the jitters coming off Rochelle: her legs beneath the table were shaking so fiercely that the cutlery was trembling.

'Jenna, she, you know, looked kinda like the girl from the café. The one who got killed.'

'You know about that?' Leighton tried to hide his surprise.

'It was on the news. She looked younger in the photograph, but I recognised her just the same.'

'And she looked like this girl, Jenna?'

'Yeah, on the night I met that girl, she called to me from across the street and I thought she was Jenna. So, then, when I heard Jenna was missing too. I thought maybe he'd got to Jenna too. I figured maybe the sicko has, like, a type, you know?'

'Well, you don't need to worry because it looks like he's locked up.'

'They're sure they've got the right guy?'

'Apparently so,' Leighton said. 'As far as I know, there was evidence linking him to the remains of the girl you met.'

Rochelle let out a long sigh, and her expression softened.

'Thank God, because I realised that me and Jenna look a lot alike too. Some of the other girls on the street thought we were sisters. So, I got to worrying that maybe he'd come after me next.'

'No, there's nothing to worry about,' Leighton said. Unaware just how wrong he was.

24

Karen Luz had finally had enough of the stench from Barney's Bar 'n' Grill. She ran a small craft shop in the town of Lakehead. It was a neat and pretty little shop, selling colourful dreamcatchers, scented candles, local pottery, and little figurines of cartoon cacti with googly eyes, wearing various outfits. She had opened the place three years earlier and it did good trade – especially during summer and fall. It probably helped that hers was the last business on the street: customers who had walked the length of the main street and wanted to make the trip worth their while usually bought something. Almost directly across the road from Karen's shop, was Barney's Bar 'n' Grill.

She had become increasingly aware of the smell in recent months. When there was a light breeze, it didn't seem too bad. But on days when the heat was rising, and the air was still, the aroma of rotting meat drifted across the street like a stinking phantom. If she closed the shop door, customers would walk on by and she would lose sales; if she left it open, the whole place would stink. What made the situation worse was that Karen's apartment was located right above the shop, so she couldn't even go home to escape the smell of decay.

Sitting on a wooden stool at the rear of her shop, she picked up the phone and called the San Diego Environmental Services.

'Hi there, I really need to speak to somebody that deals with public sanitation. I'm in Lakehead, and there's some kinda problem with the property across the street from me.' There was a pause and Karen rolled her eyes. 'Yeah, sure, I'll hold,' she said.

25

After they'd left the clatter of Ruby's diner, Leighton and Rochelle walked along the pier. The warm air blowing over the sun-bleached boardwalk was fresh and smelled of ozone.

'Do you come down here often to escape all the crazy cop shit?' Rochelle asked, as she took a pack of cigarettes from her purse.

'I used to visit here all the time about ten years ago,' Leighton said, as he gazed around nostalgically. 'When my daughter was little we would come down here every other afternoon after school. We'd mostly go to the play park over on Tyson Street.' An involuntary smile touched the corners of Leighton's mouth. 'Man, she would spend hours there. I sometimes think I enjoyed the place as much as she did. Good times.'

'But not anymore?' Rochelle asked. She could see the sadness in his eyes.

'Huh?' Her question pulled Leighton out of the past. 'No, I guess I'm not really much of a dad any more. Haven't really been for a while now.'

'How come?' Rochelle asked bluntly.

Leighton glanced at her momentarily and decided it couldn't do any harm to talk about it.

'She wants to grow up, I suppose, but to me she's still just a kid. I mean, she's already fooling around with boys and staying out all night.'

'Sounds pretty tame to me. What does her mom say?'

Leighton stopped for a moment and looked out across the restless ocean.

'She has no mom, that's partly the problem.'

'So, is there no Mrs Jones at home?'

'No, I was married once, but it didn't work out.'

'You never know, she might come back. These things happen.'

'Not this time,' Leighton said definitively.

'Why not?'

'Heather took her own life not long after our separation.'

'Shit,' Rochelle frowned. 'That must've been pretty tough.'

'Yeah, I know. That's why I try to cut her some slack – maybe too much.'

'I meant on you,' Rochelle said softly.

'I can handle it,' Leighton said, 'that's the parent's job, right?'

'Yeah? Well not in my world.'

'Do you keep in touch with your family?' Leighton asked.

'C'mon! What parent wants an addict and a hooker for a kid? It was never on the cards; no little girl grows up wanting to be like me. At least I hope they don't.'

'What did you want to be when you were a kid?'

'Loved,' Rochelle said simply.

'Tough times?'

'Other people have a worse story than mine,' Rochelle said dismissively, and Leighton thought the conversation was closed. Then, for some reason, Rochelle looked at her feet and spoke in a quiet voice, different from her usual tough persona. 'When I was a little kid, maybe seven or eight, I had this book from the school library. It was a proper hardback with a dustjacket and everything – *Little House on the Prairie* by Laura Ingalls Wilder.'

Leighton nodded. 'Like the TV show?'

'Yeah, I think that's right. But we didn't have a TV – the repo men took it away when my mom failed to make any payments on it. After dad left she didn't really know how to take care of things. Losing the TV wasn't a big deal to me, books were better. Some nights when I was too hot to sleep I would lie in my bed and read it cover to cover. I wasn't the best reader – I guess I just loved the idea of travelling through the land in that wagon, your own home on wheels. Imagine keeping on going till you find the perfect spot then building a cabin on it.'

Leighton smiled. 'So, you fancied the freedom, huh?'

'Yeah, I still do, but I guess I liked Laura in the books – she was a little fighter. And the pa in the story was the real deal. He kept his children safe and told bedtime stories and played music on his fiddle. Maybe that's what I wanted when I grew up – someone like that who would make me feel safe.' She laughed in a sad way. 'But instead I got Billy, a crack pipe, and lived unhappily ever after.'

'You're still young, Rochelle. There are good people and a whole world out there just waiting for you.'

'Not for me. I'm like a broken mirror. I sometimes wish, you know, I could go back to the start again. I don't know,' she shrugged her shoulders, 'maybe do things differently.'

'I recognise that feeling,' Leighton said softly, 'but mistakes are only a problem if we don't learn from them. You still using?'

'Every day. Just cocaine,' she said, as if it was as normal as the sun rising over California.

'You ever try to get clean?' Leighton asked.

'I will, someday,' she said with a touch of sincerity, but they avoided each other's gaze – knowing how unlikely it was that this day would ever come. 'Until then, I guess I'll be working the streets of Oceanside – whilst avoiding the Vice unit and some psycho killer.'

'Couldn't you stay off the streets until this thing is over?' Leighton asked.

'Only if I want to lose my home.'

'Look, I'll give you my cell phone number. If you can arrange for me to speak to some of the girls, maybe I can help you track down this girl Jenna. That way you can worry a bit less.'

'Sure,' Rochelle smiled, 'that would be great. I'll ask around. I'm not saying the girls will trust you, but maybe if I'm there it'll be okay. There's one girl called Danielle, she seems to be the last of the girls to have seen Jenna.'

'Fine,' Leighton said. 'You track her down and let me know. I'm available most nights.'

26

Elizabeth Walker did not notice the car at first.

After helping to close up the roadside burger bar where she worked, she had quickly taken off her black apron and cap, then stuffed them both in her purse. She then used the freshly mopped toilets to change into a tight skirt and glittery top. Elizabeth had partly hoped that when Stacey, her manager, saw her change into a party outfit she would have offered her a lift to the South side of the city. That was both where Stacey lived, and where Elizabeth's friend's twenty first birthday celebration was. However, when she emerged from the toilets Elizabeth found that Stacey was standing impatiently in the main doorway with a set of keys jangling in the lock.

'C'mon,' she said impatiently, 'it's after eleven- I'll be back in this place in eight hours from now!'

'Sorry,' Elizabeth mumbled as she clicked across the damp tiles of the floor.

Once they were both outside, Stacey locked the glass doors and said a quick goodnight to Elizabeth, before crossing the small parking lot and vanishing into her car.

It was colder outside than Elizabeth had expected. A cold wind blowing in off the dark ocean caused goose bumps to form on her bare legs.

'Selfish bitch!' Elizabeth had muttered before starting off on a journey to find the nearest bus stop.

Fortunately, it did not take her too long. She had only walked less than a quarter of a kilometre away from the closed burger bar when she found sanctuary beneath a curved bus shelter with a smooth metal bench on which to rest.

She had hoped to check the bus times, but the timetable had been replaced with an advertising poster for whale and dolphin tours. She would just have to hope a bus was due soon.

It was only after Elizabeth had glanced up and down the road in both directions that she noticed the car parked on the opposite side of the street from her. The vehicle was dark, colourless and glossy beneath the sodium lights.

Suddenly the car's lights flashed twice.

Elizabeth glanced instinctively at the vehicle for a moment, then purposely returned her attention to looking out for a bus. It was unlikely that anybody she knew would be parked around here. None of her friends from college came to this side of town – unless she was working a Saturday and they wanted a free lunch. She therefore kept her eyes locked on the road in the hope of seeing the safety of an approaching bus.

Suddenly the car lights flashed again. Longer, it seemed. There were two slow flashes. This time Elizabeth turned her face and looked at the car for longer. It was then she realised the driver of the car was frantically waving at her. It was too far away to see any features, just a figure which was clearly waving at her.

Elizabeth stood up and held a hand up to shield her eyes as she peered at the dark car.

The headlights flashed again.

In a moment of hopeful inspiration, Elizabeth realised that the driver may actually have been Stacey. Perhaps she had experienced a sudden change of heart and decided to return to pick her younger colleague up and save her from the cold blade of the wind. That would explain why the driver was waving so vigorously and trying to catch her attention.

Elizabeth tucked her purse beneath her arm and, having checked both ways on the deserted road, hurried toward the dark car.

***

It was much more difficult to drag the remains from North Santa Fe Avenue to the cliff edge, than he had imagined it would be.

The curled fingers of the burger girl kept snagging on dried shrubs and bushes as he pulled the body away from the open trunk of the car. Eventually however, after ten minutes or so, he got them to the edge. Sitting down on the dusty ground, he braced himself with his hands and used his legs to push the body over the edge of the small ravine in Guajome Regional Park. It was a struggle, but eventually the pushing and grunting gave way, and the body tumbled into infinity.

As he sat panting and sweating in the darkness, he felt the urge to drive back to the city for another one.

27

Danielle sat in McDonalds, squirming in her seat. It had taken Rochelle, who was sitting next to her, half an hour to coax her off the street.

'You sure he's not Vice?' she asked, as she nodded to where Leighton was standing at the counter. It was the third time she had directed the question toward Rochelle.

'No, he's not,' Rochelle said in a hushed voice, 'he's gonna help find Jenna.'

'Good luck,' Dannielle said dismissively. 'That girl will be lying dead in a storm drain somewhere.'

Leighton returned to the table carrying a plastic tray that was crammed with drinks, wrapped burgers and fries.

As he sat down, Rochelle divided the food between them.

'So,' Leighton said as he sat down, 'Rochelle told me that you saw Jenna on the night she vanished.'

'I said I *might* have seen her,' Danielle clarified, and began to tear into her food.

'Can you remember where she was when you *might* have seen her?'

'Down on the Boulevard. It was a quiet night, so I reckon I passed her a couple of times. Jenna was a quiet one. Some of the girls, like Rochelle here, will holler across the street if they know you – kinda looking out for each other. Jenna, she just kept her head down and did what she did.'

'Did you see anyone with her?' Leighton asked.

'Nope,' Danielle said, gathering fries into her hand.

'Were any cars nearby?'

'Are you serious? There were about two hundred cars nearby – it's a fucking highway.'

'This is a waste of time,' Leighton said, directing his attention to Rochelle. 'Enjoy your burgers, ladies.'

He stood up to leave but Rochelle grabbed his arm.

'Hang on, don't go. Danielle doesn't mean anything, she's a bitch by nature.'

'I am what the shitty world made me,' Danielle said with an indifferent shrug.

Leighton cautiously sat back down again.

'D,' Rochelle said quietly, 'the man is trying to help. Give him a goddam break, will you?'

'Did you see anything unusual that night at all?' Leighton asked in an exasperated tone.

'Well, I did see this guy, nowhere near Jenna, but he is a real asshole. I remember being kinda freaked out and thinking it was the psycho guy again.'

'What psycho guy?' Rochelle asked.

'From last year. The asshole who tried to put me in his car.'

'Oh,' Rochelle nodded vigorously as she remembered.

'What happened with this guy?' Leighton asked.

Danielle sighed indifferently, but her tone of voice betrayed her cool exterior. 'One time I was working over on Vegas Drive. I'd had a couple of tricks and was heading home. Some guy pulled over and said he would pay me double. That got me freaked right away, because nobody offers to pay double, ever – you know what I mean? It's always about paying less, not more, so it smelled like a set-up to me. I told him to forget about it and I walked away, but the next thing I know, this creep is out of his car and coming after me.'

'Prick,' Rochelle said as she crushed her burger wrapper in her hand.

'Had you seen the guy before?' Leighton asked.

'No, never,' Danielle said whilst shaking her head. 'But the freaky thing is that he started trying to hustle me into his car, and all the time he kept calling me some other name – Vera, or Violet, or some shit like that.'

'What happened? How did you get away from him?'

'Well, he kinda gripped my arm and was looking at me in this messed up way. But then Larry pulled up in his SUV and the psycho hurried back to his car and sped off.'

'Larry's your boyfriend?'

Danielle laughed bitterly.

'No,' Rochelle said patiently, 'he's her pimp.'

'The crazy thing is, Larry wasn't coming to save me, he was coming to make sure I went with the psycho.'

'Did you tell anyone about the incident at the time?' Leighton asked.

'Sure,' Danielle shrugged her shoulders, 'I even took two buses to make a police report down at the station on Mission Avenue. Waste of time and money – the pig I spoke to said that somebody would follow it up and get back to me.'

'Did they?'

'I heard nada, but it didn't faze me. No cop is going to waste time on a hooker getting beaten up, or worse.'

'That's not true,' Leighton said firmly.

'Oh, and I suppose you're a hooker, and that's how you know, right?' Danielle raised her eyebrows expectantly.

'No,' Leighton said defiantly, 'but I'm a cop.'

'Well I guess that puts you on the other side of the fence from me, so you know shit about what we do!'

'D, he's just trying to help,' Rochelle said in a voice that was close to pleading.

'Yeah, or maybe he's just sniffing around for a promotion,' Danielle eyed Rochelle from head to toe. 'Or maybe he's sniffing around something else.'

Rochelle shook her head in exasperation, but Leighton ignored the accusation and continued with his line of questioning.

'Did you provide a description of the guy who grabbed you, in your report?'

'Sure, I even gave the license plate of his car – for all the good it did. The guy I spoke to looked at me like I was a diseased dog.'

This particular detail got Leighton's attention. In his experience, descriptions from witnesses were often sketchy at best. Definite details like plates, street names, and numbers, were generally more reliable.

'You gave the license plate in your police report?' he asked, to confirm the fact.

'That's what I said, didn't I?' Danielle said, before she drained the last of her Coke and stood up. 'Okay, I'm done here. The way I see it, the guy could be driving around here, taking another girl every night, and no one would give a shit. Later, Chelle.'

'Thanks,' Leighton said, but Danielle ignored him and strutted to the door.

After her friend had gone, Rochelle looked at Leighton apologetically.

'Sorry about that. Danielle's usually less of a bitch.'

'To you maybe,' Leighton smiled. 'I guess I'm more of a threat.'

'Well, the Vice cops we meet from the Special Enforcement section aren't always full of respect. Danielle has probably seen a decade of abuse.'

'Fair enough. Listen, can you remember if she told you at the time that she had been attacked?'

'Yeah,' Rochelle said, 'she spoke to all the girls on our corner, just to give them a heads-up.'

'That's good. Can you remember when that was?'

'Last year. I think it was near Christmas because I remember when D was telling me about it, she was wearing these little flashing reindeer earrings.'

'Okay', Leighton nodded. 'What's Danielle's surname?'

Rochelle looked at him blankly. 'I've no idea,' she said.

'But I thought you'd known her for a while?'

'I have – four years, give or take.'

'And you don't know her name?'

'No, why would I? We just work the same streets. Like people who wait on the same bus stop every morning. You might nod to each other, and maybe even speak a little, but telling people your name – your real name – especially on the streets, nobody has that much trust in anyone out there; names are a big deal. But I guess it might make a difference to your searching.'

'Yeah, it makes looking for the report a bit trickier without a surname, but I'll see what I can do.' Leighton looked at his watch. 'Look, I need to check in at the station. Can I drop you somewhere?'

'No, it's cool,' Rochelle said with a shrug. 'I'm due to start work now anyway.' She stood up, pulled a tin of lip gloss from her purse and used a finger to smear it across her puckered mouth. 'Thanks for helping us out,' she said, almost absently, but Leighton could see the gratitude in her expression.

'It's nothing,' Leighton smiled.

'No rest for the wicked,' she said. Something in her eyes suggested that she meant it.

After Rochelle had gone, Leighton took a small notepad from his pocket and scribbled down a few details.

When he stepped out of the clinical glare of the burger bar, into the night, Leighton had to narrow his eyes in the darkness. The air was mild, and some cicadas mirrored the sound of his feet as he walked across the parking lot to his car. The area was hemmed in by a low wall on one side and a cardboard-waste compacter on the other. He had parked in the back corner of the lot, where it would be less obvious to Gretsch's spies.

Leighton had just reached the door of his car when the attack came.

The figure, dressed in dark clothes, stepped from the shadows and cracked Leighton on the back of the head with a tire iron. A flash of pain eclipsed his thoughts. As he fell forward against the side of the car, the figure hit him again, this time on his back. Then it crouched down and spoke to him.

'Back off from my business or I'll put you in the ground,' it whispered. The figure punched Leighton hard in the face then melted into the night, leaving him groaning in agony on the asphalt.

Eventually, he gripped the side of the door and levered himself up. He reached up to his head and felt around his scalp for blood. Fortunately, there was only a painful swelling.

He glanced around, hoping to find some witnesses, but the brightness inside the burger bar meant that the numerous diners would see nothing through the large glass windows but darkness and their own reflections.

28

As he limped into the office area at the back of Oceanside Police Station, Leighton found a dozen or so officers dotted around the room. Most were typing into computers, or phoning around to follow up leads on one case or another. His colleagues that were speaking on the telephone looked much more relaxed than those typing up reports.

'Hey, day shift's over, Jonesy. You not heading home?' one of them called out.

'You know, I was going to head off for a shower and a cool beer,' Leighton smiled, 'but then I figured, why do that when I could crawl back here and enjoy some paperwork – just for the fun of it, you realise.'

'True that,' the other man said amiably as he glanced round at Leighton. He did a double take when he saw his swollen eye. 'Hey, what happened to you, Jonesy – did you get hit by a truck?'

'Sure feels like it. Some guy attacked me outside the drive thru on—' Leighton winced.

'Maybe you should get yourself checked out?' the man said, returning his attention to his screen.

As Leighton eased himself into his chair, he winced at the flash of pain that ripped across his back. He waited, frozen still, for the burning tide to finally ebb away. If the attacker had hoped that his assault on Leighton would frighten him off, he was mistaken: it'd had the opposite effect. He now knew the killer was real, and if he was real he could be stopped. The first step would be locating Danielle's report – if it existed – and extracting any details from it.

Leighton exhaled and dragged his hands over his eyes; finding Danielle's report could be tricky. If the report had been made this year it would have been on the new, computerised reporting and logging system, and Leighton could have searched for information by anything from incident type to zip code. However, if Rochelle's estimation was correct, and the attempted abduction had taken place in the previous winter, the report would be filed as a paper copy. That meant he would have to wade through the mountain of files in the basement.

He got up from his desk and crossed the work area to the glass door at the far end of the room. Descending the concrete stairs that lead to the records room, Leighton tried to smooth out the creases in his shirt. He always felt a bit scruffy when he encountered the records technician, Angela, who was friendly, but meticulous in her organisation of the subterranean domain.

At the bottom of the stairs Leighton entered a large open-plan area, which was surrounded by six rows of ten filing shelves. The central space was dominated by a large wooden table, covered in piles of cardboard wallet folders. At the far end of the room, a tall woman was busily peeling sheets of paper from a large pile, placing each sheet in one of four flatbed document scanners.

'Hey, Angela, you working night shifts now?'

The woman turned and peered at Leighton over the top of her glasses.

'Oh, hi, Jonesy. Yeah, the switch-over to digital records is still a physical job – no rest for the wicked, eh? What happened to your face, did the captain do that?' she asked with a knowing smile.

'He wishes. No, it was just some random attack. I got punched coming out of a burger bar. You got a pile of paperwork there,' Leighton said, deliberately shifting the conversation away from his injury.

'I sure do. It grows bigger every day. Lisa and I are working our way through each month but it's a slow process. Every record has to be scanned – front and back. Anyway, what brings you down here, got a court hearing to prepare for?'

'No,' Leighton shook his head, 'thankfully. I just wanted to take a look at a report that came in last year.'

'Sure, you got a case number?' Angela asked.

'No, sorry,' he said, and offered an apologetic smile.

Angela looked at him and frowned like a teacher who's been told by a pupil that they've forgotten their homework.

'Well, have you got a plate, or vehicle identification number?'

'No, it's not a traffic incident.'

'No? So, what's your interest if it's not traffic?' Angela was a woman who liked things to be neat, and having a traffic officer look at a non-traffic report was not neat.

Leighton was caught momentarily off balance and was unsure of what to say. But the awkward question was avoided when a buzzer rang, signalling that somebody was upstairs at the public records window hatch.

'You know what, I'm too busy to even care. Lisa has gone home sick, morning sickness probably, so I have to cover the desk upstairs too. Do you even know what month the report was made?' she asked hopefully.

'Yes,' Leighton said, pleased to have something definite – at least he hoped it was. 'The report came in during December.'

'Well, I'm scanning my way through July of last year right now. If you can wait a couple of weeks you'll be able to look it up on the system; otherwise, you're going to have to make a manual search yourself I'm afraid.'

'I'm fine with leafing through the paperwork – remember, I'm old school through and through.'

Angela leaned over to her desk and pressed a button on the scanner. It clicked to life and began to hum.

The buzzer rang again.

'Okay,' she said, 'December of last year is in that shelving unit there.' She pointed to a tall grey structure at the end of the room. It was filled with rows of multi-coloured document wallets. 'You already know the third row is traffic, right?'

'Yeah.' Leighton nodded.

'Well, general crime is the two rows above that; serious assault, sexual crime and homicide are below, and the bottom row is missing persons. They're arranged by date so don't mess up my system.'

'I won't,' Leighton smiled. 'I promise. Thanks for letting me do this.'

The buzzer rang for the third time.

'Jeez, I'm coming!' Angela growled, and vanished out of the room.

It took Leighton over an hour to find the report he was looking for. A couple of times he'd got excited when he found the phrase 'attempted abduction' in the incident description box. However, in both cases it turned out to be a divorced parent trying to see their kid during the holiday season. One of them, which was familiar to the entire station, had involved a recently separated dad who had apparently met his twelve-year-old kid outside school, and taken him to McDonalds on Atlantic Avenue to hand over some Christmas gifts. The guy had told the kid's childminder what he was doing and that he would drop the kid home afterwards. The concerned mother had made a phone call, alleging that an abduction had taken place, and the festive father found himself cuffed, face down on the floor of the burger bar, with four officers aiming locked and loaded handguns at him.

Eventually, Leighton opened a document folder to see the name Danielle underneath the incident description of assault/ attempted abduction.

He sat on the floor of the records area and held the stapled white sheets of paper in his hand, peering at them. The document confirmed that the report had been made the week before Christmas. The name recorded was Miss Danielle Millar, age twenty-three, her occupation was marked as unemployed, but someone had written the word prostitute beneath this. Her address was listed as the Four Seasons RV and Caravan Park.

The report stated that the victim was propositioned at 11pm. by a dark haired, Caucasian male in a red Toyota. When she rejected his advances, he'd got out of his vehicle and pursued her along the street – at which point he attempted to force her into his vehicle. The recording officer had written that it was a possible case of mistaken identity, as the victim said the alleged perpetrator had called her Veronica at various points during the altercation. Leighton took a small notebook from his chest pocket and wrote down the report number and the licence plate.

There were two things in particular that concerned him about the report. The first was that in the box titled action taken, a simple pen mark had been slashed across the page. This suggested that the incident required no further investigation. The second – and perhaps more alarming – was the fact that the officer who had made the report was Detective Slater.

Angela returned just as Leighton was struggling to slot his final three document wallets into their respective locations.

'It's okay,' she said, 'you can leave those last ones with me – they'll all have to come out to get scanned anyway.'

'Thanks, Angela, I appreciate this,' Leighton said, and he meant it.

'Did you find what you were looking for?' she asked.

'Yeah, I reckon so,' Leighton replied, but gave nothing else away.

'Good,' Angela said, her hands on her hips, 'because I am done here too. Would you believe I've been here since 8am? So, the rest of the filing can wait until morning. In any case, you look like you could do with getting a rest too.'

'I will,' Leighton said. 'I just have some paperwork to finish first.'

29

He gripped the tooth in the steel pliers, held it up to the light, and peered at it. Now that it had been properly cleaned, it was a thing of beauty. He placed it in the small glass dish with the others. At first there had only been that one, small premolar, like an ivory seed. But now, thanks to his nocturnal activities, there were three of them. It was better, yet not quite enough. Not yet.

That was why the move from the small town of Lakehead to the city of Oceanside had been necessary. There were so many girls on the streets here, which meant the chance of seeing another Veronica was high. And, with so many of them lingering on dark corners, and crawling around pool halls, nobody would miss a few of them.

The urge had consumed him the previous evening. As he'd slid into the driver's seat of his car, he had told himself it was just for a drive, but he knew what he was doing. He'd cruised backwards and forwards along the Boulevard, and that was when he'd seen her: the one who got away. At first, he'd thought his mind was just blurring past and present, like it did when he saw one who resembled Veronica, but this was no trick of the mind; it was the same girl.

She was his first attempt when he had arrived in the city. She had struggled and fought in a way he hadn't expected. Now that he was more skilled, he would know how to subdue her, but not back then. He had panicked, and some hero in an SUV showed up, forcing him to flee without his prize. The worst part was that he had left two witnesses behind.

That bitch had made him change his car. He had taken it to the Rollins Stock Cars dealership and traded it in. The salesman had wittered on about mileage, but he hadn't been listening. Instead, he had gazed around at the anonymous vehicles and realised, if he wanted to keep killing, he should take cars from places like that. He never did take a car from that particular lot – it was just a little too close to home. However, he did dump one there.

Tonight, he planned to go for another drive, to make sure that the one who'd got away came home where she belonged.

30

Sitting back in his chair, Leighton winced at the throbbing pain in his head. His hand instinctively moved to the area of injury, where his fingers found a painful, swollen bulge. He rummaged through his desk drawer until he found a small blister pack of painkillers. He popped out two white pills and washed them down with a gulp of cold coffee, shaking his head against the combined bitter tastes.

Glancing between his notepad and the screen, Leighton opened up the database and keyed in the licence plate number to check it against the DMV records. After he hit the enter button, he watched as lines of information filled the screen.

The zip code in the top corner of the screen indicated that the vehicle was registered to a Californian resident. When their name appeared – Michael Stanton – it was marked in red, which indicated that he had been given a conviction, suspension or revocation. Leighton scanned to the bottom of the screen where a box provided further information, which specified that Stanton was a convicted felon. A photograph in the corner of the screen showed an awkward looking teenager, trying to appear defiant as he stared into the lens of the police camera. However, his stated age was thirty-nine. Leighton frowned and stared at the information on the screen.

The youthful face in the photograph made more sense to Leighton when he realised that Stanton had served time for unlawful killing back in 1987. Having spent nineteen years in jail, he had been released in May 2005 – less than a year and a half earlier.

If Danielle was correct, and this was the guy who'd attacked her, he had been off the streets for almost two decades after he'd originally become a killer. Leighton believed in rehabilitation, and possibly even redemption, but not for everyone. Some killers were fixed on a path that they would never step off. Stanton may be like that: perhaps he had stopped killing whilst incarcerated and simply needed to catch up once released.

Leighton scrolled down the screen to reveal the details of his original crime. Michael Stanton was convicted of the unlawful killing of Steven Cooper and his daughter Veronica. The record indicated that both victims had died in a house fire, which had been started deliberately by Stanton.

Leighton shook his head at the idea of it and rubbed his temples.

The registered address listed was also the home address of the vehicle owner, in the town of Lakehead, San Diego.

After adjusting himself in his chair, and scribbling down some details, Leighton began tapping on the computer keyboard again. This time he brought up a selection of archived newspaper reports on the events surrounding the death of the Coopers. Leighton's eyes widened in horror as he read exactly what had happened two decades earlier.

31

Danielle's feet were starting to hurt as she limped home. The previous afternoon she had picked up a pair of pink stilettos, from a sale rack in town, for ten bucks. The cheap shoes were a size too large, but this hadn't seemed a problem when she'd initially tried them on around her apartment. However, after a night of trudging the sidewalks of Oceanside, the stiff edge of the shoes had rubbed a raw sore on both of Danielle's heels. Eventually, she slipped the shoes off and carried them in one hand as she walked along the desolate streets, lined with tall palm trees.

At 3.15am. the roads were mostly deserted. However, within moments a dark car appeared along the empty street behind Danielle. As it drew level with her, two young men laughed and shouted obscenities from the anonymity of a half-rolled-down window. As the car gleefully revved away from her, Danielle responded with a gesture of her own: she stuck up her middle finger.

'Couple of real fucking heroes, aren't you?'

Suddenly, she felt a jolt of pain in her foot. Looking down, Danielle discovered that she had stepped on to the glistening debris of a smashed beer bottle. Dropping her shoes, she tilted her left foot up to her right knee, making her look like a dislocated flamingo. Upon inspection, she found there was a small, sparkling wedge of glass protruding from the filthy ball of her foot. She gripped the sliver with her plastic nails and pulled it from her skin.

'Fuck!' She winced as she put her foot down on the grimy sidewalk.

It was painful, but she figured she could still walk on it. It seemed like her only option; especially as she was only fifteen minutes from home, and if she called Larry and woke him up, he would give her more than a painful foot. She was committed to making the difficult journey home.

As she glanced up ahead, Danielle saw that the dark car had stopped at the roadside, its brake lights glowing like angry red eyes; she knew that walking past the car would not be a good idea. One person would be easy enough to fight off, but two would be harder – especially with a busted foot.

Despite her painful feet and her desire to get home, Danielle turned around and walked along the sidewalk in the opposite direction. As her bare feet slapped against the ground, she glanced over her shoulder and saw that the dark car had not moved. That was when she realised that those two young men might have been involved in Jen's disappearance. She shuddered in fear. What if the asshole who had attempted to kidnap her had got himself a partner? She glanced over her shoulder a second time.

Thankfully, she saw a comforting sight up ahead. At the edge of the road, an old Toyota saloon was parked up, and a blonde woman appeared to be trying to change a wheel. She was crouched on one knee with a tyre iron beside her.

'Here, I can help you,' Danielle said as she approached the woman.

'I know you can,' said a deep voice, and the woman turned, revealing a masculine face beneath an unconvincing wig.

Before Danielle could react, a Taser sent a bolt of crackling electricity through her body and she crumpled to the ground. She continued to shudder and twitch as the man in the bad wig picked her up and dropped her into the open trunk.

A short while later Danielle's body, still warm, was lifted out of the car. Once it was inside the house, the man who had taken her knelt on Daniel's chest and got busy with her face.

32

The morning sun was already warm, and the air was getting hotter by the minute, when Leighton met Danny in the car park of the station. It was 8.15am. and various teams of officers, from patrol, harbour, and traffic, were leaving the building to start the day watch. Danny had left a message for Leighton, to tell him that his sister and brother-in-law were planning to spend the day at the hospital before heading back to Reno. This respite meant that Danny could complete a normal shift without sneaking around or making complicated plans.

'So, you all set, or has it been too long?' Leighton asked him as they ambled toward the cruiser.

'You better remind me what we got today, Jonesy. It gets a bit jumbled when you've been out of the loop.'

'Don't worry, it's an easy one – just a DUI check over on College Boulevard.'

'Easy maybe, but if it's as quiet as last week it's going to be a long day.'

'I'd take a slow shift over a mountain of paperwork any day,' Leighton said with a smile.

'Well, I could try to only pull over the drivers who look sober?' Danny offered.

After laying out a lane of orange cones, Leighton and Danny placed four yellow warning signs, thirty feet apart, along the edge of the road. The purpose of this was to guide selected vehicles out of the stream of traffic to a stopping point, where the drivers could be checked by either of the officers. They took turns to guide the selected cars to the checking area and administer the breath test.

The morning was as uneventful as had been expected – the majority of drunks were usually caught late afternoon and early evening. Most offenders were those who had decided to wash down their lunch with a couple of beers and drive back to work, or, more usually, home. Every driver the two officers stopped that morning was reassuringly sober.

At lunchtime Danny walked half a mile to the market on the corner of Highway 76, and returned with chilled water and packets of sandwiches, which he and Leighton devoured as they sat on the tailgate of the cruiser.

'Pretty low hit rate,' Danny said, as he sipped from his bottle. 'The captain will give us hell for underperformance again.'

'It's early yet,' Leighton said, 'plus, Gretsch will give us hell regardless.'

'I suppose.' Danny shrugged. 'You managing to keep yourself from sniffing around that case?'

'Almost,' Leighton said with a wry smile.

'I suspected as much.'

'You know me too well,' Leighton said, as he watched the rumbling traffic on the freeway.

'What have you got?' Danny asked.

'Nothing concrete, but I found this incident involving a working girl who may have been caught up in a failed abduction by the same guy.'

'Where?'

'Here in Oceanside.'

'Wow.' Danny blew out a whistle of air. 'How did you find out?'

'I did some digging in the station records last night.'

'Was there a report on the abduction?'

'Yeah, but here's the thing – no action was ever taken, not follow up, nothing. Doesn't that stink?'

'It sure does. Who filed the report?' Danny asked.

'Guess,' Leighton said.

'The captain?'

'Close. It was Slater.'

'Whoa, you sure you want to go there, Jonesy? That would be playing with a loaded gun. If Slater knew you'd been sniffing around his reports, he'd go straight to Gretsch.'

'Don't I know it. But what about the lack of follow up? I thought Slater was strictly by the book.'

'Nah,' said Danny, shaking his head. 'It makes all kinds of sense. Slater worked Vice before he moved to Homicide. Richie Fallens told me that Slater got transferred out of Vice after a street walker complained about him.'

'Ah,' said Leighton, nodding, 'a small man with a big grudge.'

'Yeah, that's one officer who will be quite happy to see ladies of the night in danger.'

'So, it looks like I'm stuck with nowhere to go.'

'Well you might as well sit back and enjoy your lunch.'

'Amen, partner.'

It was almost 2.30pm. when the man in the Lexus pointed the loaded gun at Leighton's chest: he had been pulled over only moments earlier. Danny had waved his car into the inspection lane where Leighton was waiting. The first indication that anything was wrong was the man leaving his engine running when he'd pulled up next to Leighton. He was in his early fifties, balding, and dressed in a light grey suit. A thin sheen of sweat was visible on his brow, but it was a hot day so that did not particularly alarm Leighton.

'Please turn off the engine, sir,' Leighton said, as he began noting down the make and model of the car. When he glanced up from his notepad, Leighton realised that the driver had raised his hand to the car key but he had not actually touched it. His hand was simply hovering in the air, as if he were attempting a magic spell.

'Sir,' Leighton repeated in a more assertive manner, 'turn off the engine, now.'

'What? Oh yes, sorry,' the man said, smiling nervously. This time he did turn off the engine, but his expression was pained. If

Leighton had been less distracted, or closer to him, he may have detected the sharp stench of spirit on the man's breath.

'Can I please see your driver's license and registration documents?'

'No,' the man said in the tone of a petulant child. His hands were fastened on the steering wheel and Leighton could see the veins starting to bulge on the back of them.

'Okay, sir, step out of the vehicle. Don't worry, you're not in any trouble.'

'I know.' He grinned. 'You're the one in trouble. With your shitty little tests and penalties. Why can't a guy have a couple of bourbons if he wants?'

Leighton glanced up from his notepad to see the man leaning out of the car window, pointing a glossy black pistol directly at his chest.

'Okay there, buddy,' Leighton said in a calm voice, slowly placing his hands in the air. 'Let's just relax and we can sort this situation out.'

'I'm not your "buddy",' the sweating man said. 'Now take your gun out of your holster and put it down on the goddam ground.'

'Sure,' Leighton said, 'whatever you say.'

Leighton very slowly and deliberately removed his gun from his holster and placed it on the ground. It was at that moment, Danny – who was twenty feet away at the start of the cones – glanced over at his partner and noticed that something wasn't right. He began walking toward him.

The man glanced over at Danny approaching them, and in that moment, Leighton took his chance. In one slick movement, he gripped his baton, which was attached to his belt on the opposite side from his pistol, and detached it from its clip. As he swung it upwards the baton extended out, allowing all three steel sections to slide and click solidly into place. He swung the steel rod down, smashing it into his assailant's hand. The gun clattered to the ground. The man screamed in pain as Leighton crouched and recovered both weapons. As he stood up, he holstered his own gun and smiled courteously.

'Once again, sir,' Leighton said, as he instinctively brought his hand to his belt, 'please step out of the vehicle.'

This time, the man complied.

After the driver had been tested – confirming he was four times over the legal limit – he was cuffed and removed by a mobile unit. Leighton and Danny were left to gather up the cones as the evening traffic surged past them.

'So, Jonesy, that was a pretty little baton move you had back there,' Danny said, as they carried their respective orange burdens back to the open trunk of the cruiser.

'Yeah,' Leighton shrugged. 'I guess I prefer it to firing a pistol.'

'How come?'

'Well, it's less lethal and it requires much less paperwork to be filled in if I ever use it.'

'I'll go with that,' Danny nodded.

'You want me to drop you off at the hospital?' Leighton asked.

'No thanks. My sister will be there until ten. If you drop me off at the station it'll give me a chance to show my face around the place. Show the rest of the guys that I still exist. Plus, that way I can write up today's events and save you having to do it.'

'That sounds like a plan,' Leighton said, as he pressed on his key fob to unlock the car.

The two officers placed the last of the cones in the trunk of the cruiser and climbed into the vehicle.

After Leighton had dropped Danny at the station, he decided to make a stop on his way home. Without any deliberate intention, he found himself driving down to the pier again.

It was a warm evening, and a good opportunity to take a walk in the fresh air. Watching people in and around the shore was always life-affirming – it reminded him that the world wasn't entirely full of darkness. Sometimes, if he was lucky, he would find a live music rehearsal taking place in the amphitheatre that was nestled alongside the pier, and he would sit in the back row – a tired cop in a shirt and chinos – listening with his eyes closed.

Tonight, he figured a walk by the shore might help him navigate a path through the evidence he had gathered so far. He felt there was a pattern emerging, but he was too tangled up in it all to see it clearly.

As he pulled his car into the roadside, his cell phone rang. He picked it up and pressed the green button.

'Hello?' Leighton said.

'Jonesy, it's Danny. Listen, I was just grabbing a coffee in the lounge and I heard from Owen in Homicide that they got an identification on the Jane Doe found out at Lake Tanner. Her name was Jenna Dodds; don't know if that means anything to you or not?'

'Shit.' Leighton dragged a hand across his weary eyes. 'Yeah, that's the missing girl I mentioned.'

'What you going to do with it?'

'I don't know,' Leighton said, and it was the truth.

'But nothing stupid, right?'

Leighton could hear the concern in Danny's voice.

'Yeah, nothing stupid. Thanks, partner.'

After the call was over, Leighton looked out of his car window to the ocean. On the horizon, distant waves were rolling endlessly over each other. It seemed more than a coincidence that two bodies, of similar young women, had been found within a couple of days of each other. Yet, until he knew the cause of death, Leighton was unwilling to go down that particular rabbit hole. The only way to know for sure was to speak to an expert.

Leighton pulled into the parking lot of the medical examiner's office. From the outside, the orange and cream coloured building looked more like a modern office than a centre of scientific investigation. Only the brooding steel doors at the side – where the bodies would be brought in – suggested there was something serious going on behind the bright facade.

The last time he had visited, the young man on reception had taken one look at Leighton's badge and directed him to the lab where Nina worked; this time it was different.

When he approached the reception, a stern woman with glossy black hair flashed Leighton a steely smile.

'Good evening, sir, what can we do for you?'

'My name is Leighton Jones, I'm with Oceanside PD,' he said, and showed her his badge. 'I was hoping to speak to Nina Shindel – if she's available.'

There was a shift in the facial expression of the receptionist. It was nothing explicit, just a flicker, but enough to indicate to Leighton that something was wrong.

'I'm afraid that's not possible.' The receptionist's tone implied he had just asked to speak to Santa Claus.

'Why not?' Leighton asked.

'What was it that you wanted to speak to Ms Shindel about?'

'I'm not at liberty to discuss that. It's a police matter.'

At that moment Leighton heard somebody approaching him from behind and turned to see a small man with a shaved head. He was wearing a lab coat and was peeling off a pair of blue latex gloves.

'Is there a problem here?' the man asked.

'No problem,' Leighton said. 'I'm an officer with Oceanside PD. I was hoping to speak to Nina.'

'Ms Shindel no longer works in this department. My name is Ronald Freil, I'm the senior examiner here; perhaps there's something I can help you with?'

'I was just looking for a couple of details regarding the body found at Lake Tanner.'

'Are you part of the investigating team assigned to the investigation?'

'No,' Leighton sighed, 'I was just—'

'Then absolutely not.' The man held up both hands dramatically, as if in an attempt to stop an invisible train. 'I'm sorry, we can't help you.'

'Look, I'm not trying to step into anyone else's yard here, I simply know this case has elements that extend into my jurisdiction.'

The man's expression remained fixed. 'That makes no difference,' he said. 'All requests for information must go through the appropriate channels, Officer Jones.'

Leighton looked at the man for a moment, taking in how much he was enjoying the power. This was somebody who appeared too confident with their decisions to be making them alone. Coupled with the fact that Leighton had not actually given this man his name, it told him everything he needed to know.

'You're quite right,' Leighton said. 'I'm sorry to have disturbed you. I just thought for a moment that we were on the same side.'

'There are no sides,' the small man said, 'only procedures.'

'Nice mantra,' Leighton said, 'but can you do one thing for me?'

'Possibly.'

'Say hi to Captain Gretsch for me, next time he calls to pat your head and give you instructions,' Leighton said, and walked out of reception.

As he sat in his car outside the medical examiner's office, flicking through his notebook, it seemed to Leighton that the doors of this case were rapidly closing; he might have to let the matter go completely. If the universe was throwing barriers in his way, perhaps he should respect them. But part of him kept thinking about those poor women, walking the streets each night. Their lives were difficult and dangerous enough without adding a sick serial killer into the mix. He also kept thinking about Steven Cooper and his daughter Veronica. In his mind, they were a father and daughter pair, much like Leighton and Annie, until some psycho had crept up and torched their home. If Stanton was killing again, he had to be stopped.

Leighton concluded that his only real option was to get up early the following morning and take a drive out to the town of

Lakehead. Maybe if he could speak to the only survivor of the Cooper's house fire, he would see the pattern more clearly.

He climbed out of the car, leaned on the side of the bonnet and glanced over at the play park where a young couple were helping their toddler into a brightly coloured swing. He envied their life: the potential they had to make the right decisions.

Sighing, he pulled out his cell phone and shifted his attention to the nearby ocean.

Using one finger, he clumsily typed in the message:

Hey Annie – you coming back over tonight? We need to get along better. I could order some pizza. Let me know. Dad x

Slipping his phone into a pocket, Leighton crossed the road to the pier. The place was busy with lovers, and families sharing ice cream, enjoying the fading warmth of the evening. As he sat on one of the benches, Leighton gazed at the hypnotic shifting waves of the ocean and felt an overwhelming sense of loneliness.

His cell phone buzzed, pulling him from his thoughts. He glanced at it and smiled as he saw that Annie had replied. He felt a flicker of happiness. Then he read the message:

Srry, gt plans for tnght. Will call l8r. A

As he closed the phone, Leighton had to fight the urge to throw it off the pier into the shifting waves.

When he returned home that evening, Leighton lay in his bathtub and tried to make sense of the world. Perhaps if Heather had lived, he could have been a better father, and possibly a better cop. At least then he would have had somebody to talk things through with – both personally and professionally – at the end of each day. Instead, he felt as if he was always facing some kind of opposition. His daughter thought he was a loser, his boss wanted rid of him, and, despite the fact that there was a killer sneaking around Oceanside, Leighton felt powerless to stop them.

He reached to the side of the bathtub to pick up a towel and dragged it across his face. He recalled how, a decade earlier, the grief counsellor had told him in an annoyingly calm voice that life was about looking forwards – to consider where you could change things – rather than dwelling on a painful past that couldn't be altered.

Leighton thought about this advice carefully. If he were to make a difference with Annie, he would have to somehow bridge the gulf between them. Invest some time in their relationship. Gretsch would never be his greatest fan, but perhaps, if Leighton could just help Danny through the next couple of weeks, he could focus on filling in spreadsheets and giving the captain the kind of results he valued, and be a better cop.

Before he fell asleep that night, Leighton lay down on top of his bed and switched on his bedside radio. He wasn't a fan of the various talk stations, preferring instead to drift off to the sound of music. Turning the dial on the radio, he moved between the swell and fade of different stations. Snatches of tunes and conversation merged together as Leighton yawned. However, he cocked his head in interest when he tuned into the familiar twang of Muddy Waters. Smiling, Leighton lay back on the bed and closed his eyes. He knew the tune Manish Boy and was happy to have found it. As the song played, he found his thoughts drifting to a simpler period of time when he spent sunny childhood days watching his father strip engines in their small front yard.

However, when the song ended, the hourly news report brought Leighton back to cold reality:

This evening, Oceanside Police, investigating a series of homicides in the area, have arrested a suspect in the case. The killings have been dubbed the work of The Dentist after a police source confirmed that a number of victims were missing teeth. In other news, a new retail development is to be built...

'Jeez,' Leighton sighed and stared at the cheap fan on his ceiling. Whoever was passing details to the media was making investigating the case much more difficult. When key details were released to the public, countless hoax calls would come in from idiots claiming to be the killer, whilst the real one could be missed because of the process of investigating the hoaxers. And the media had given him a name too, as if being able to label a monster made it somehow less frightening. This made Leighton smile as he vaguely remembered the grief therapist telling him that expressing our anxieties in words was the first step to releasing them. The name- *The Dentist*- made little difference to Leighton's perception of the killer. He was simply a dangerous psychopath, hidden away like a snake beneath a rock, in some shadowy corner of the state.

As he let his eyes slip closed again, Leighton found himself hoping the visit to Lakehead would shine some light into that shadowy corner.

33

Danny had been sitting beside his father's hospital bed for just over an hour, when he realised he was starting to drift off himself. Leighton had dropped him at the hospital just after 8am. They were both meant to be working a half shift until noon, monitoring traffic around the city. Leighton had said that he would spend a couple of hours in the harbour area, then head over to Vandergrift Boulevard. This was one of the main roads running north out of the city. If he parked up there, when the shift was over he could easily drive the thirty-two miles up to Lakehead.

Prior to waking, Danny had been dreaming that he was back in his childhood home again, or at least a dream version of it, with secret doorways that led to interconnected rooms. There was something both familiar and unfamiliar about the place. In the dream, he had found an attic which had never existed in reality. It was full of various toys from his childhood. They were all boxed up, and the boxes were piled in dusty corners like a long-forgotten shop display. Even in the thrill of the dream, Danny knew it couldn't be real. His childhood treasure, a model of the Millennium Falcon, was there in a long box, but he remembered being away at college when his mom told him that she had cleared out his old room and tossed away the junk from under his bed. When he'd asked about the model, she said that she'd given it to a kid who lived down the block from them. Danny had felt ridiculously hurt, and embarrassed by his emotion, at the time, but his mom hadn't understood. And yet, despite the fuss, here it was, leaning against Buckaroo and his first proper bike. That was how he knew the experience wasn't real, but Danny moved toward it just as eagerly as if it had been. Perhaps, he believed, if he could just reach the box, and grasp the model tight enough, he could bring it back to reality when he surfaced. Yet as his bare feet crossed the dusty floorboards of the attic, the surface suddenly felt soft and he began to sink into the wood with the consistency of marshmallow. He stared down, wide-eyed, and watched the knots in the wood as they stretched and melted into strange spirals.

Eventually, he woke to find himself in the baking heat of the hospital ward, by his father's bedside. His father remained blissfully asleep, a small mask providing him with fresh oxygen. His hair looked wispy and his chest was barely rising and falling.

Danny touched his hand.

'Hey, Pop, I'm just going to grab a coffee,' he said. 'I'm not much use to you if I just sit here snoring.'

He left the small room and made his way past the brightly-lit nurse's station, toward the cluster of buzzing vending machines at the far end of the corridor. As he drew level with the reception desk, one of the nurses glanced up at him.

'Oh, Mr Clark, somebody called, asking for you earlier. It was about an hour ago. I came along and looked in, but you were sleeping. I figured you could probably do with the rest.'

Danny frowned. 'It's not a problem. Who was it that called?'

'A man. They didn't leave their name, sorry, but they said they'd catch up with you later.'

'Thanks,' Danny said, and wandered a little confused to the machine. Perhaps Leighton had wanted to ask him something or update him on his weird case.

After rummaging in his trouser pockets, Danny counted out the coins, slotted them in the machine, and selected a cappuccino. Eventually, when the humming and trickling had stopped, he crouched down and removed the warm cup from the machine.

As he turned around, with his dripping coffee cup in his hand, Danny found himself facing a familiar figure.

'Hello, Officer Clark,' Gretsch said with a self-satisfied smile. 'I just thought I'd take a drive over to let you know that you and your idiotic partner are in some serious shit.'

34

The nurse who met Leighton at the white wooden stairs that lead into the Golden Cross Care Home seemed particularly welcoming. She smiled broadly and gripped the officer's hand as she led him into the colonial style building.

'Now, I must let you know that Mrs Cooper doesn't get many visitors anymore,' she said. Something in her tone of voice suggested that *many* probably meant *any* visitors.

'Did she ever have many?' Leighton asked.

'Oh yes, she had weekly visits for a few years, but they stopped and then nobody came. I think she is perhaps happier that way.'

'Not so good,' Leighton said.

'It's possibly for the best. Visits seemed to upset her, especially the later ones. To be honest, I'm not sure if she'll even speak to you.'

'It's okay, I'm just following leads. No pressure either way.' Leighton smiled disarmingly.

'That's good,' the nurse said with a sigh.

'Is she in a separate room?' Leighton asked. Given the subject matter he wished to discuss, he was hoping for a little privacy.

'No, she's currently resting in the day room. But you won't be interrupted; the other residents are all outside. We try to give them as much fresh air and sunshine as we can – it tends to reduce depression and insomnia. But Mrs Cooper doesn't like being in the sunlight, or too much heat. Understandable I suppose, given what happened to her. Anyway, we're here.' The nurse stopped outside a large white door and held it open for Leighton.

'I'll be at the reception desk, if you need me,' she said.

'Thank you,' Leighton said.

As Leighton stepped into the spacious day room of the care home, he found that it was empty except for a solitary woman. Her lack of motion meant that she could easily be missed. She sat in a white wicker rocking chair, which had been positioned beside a window at the far side of the room. Crossing the room, which smelled of lavender and cafeteria food, Leighton glanced absently at the numerous bookcases crammed with Western paperbacks and colourful board games. It didn't seem such a bad place to end up.

Nearing the woman, Leighton discovered that she was looking out at the other residents of the care home, who were enjoying a picnic on a large lawn at the rear of the building.

'Mrs Cooper?' Leighton said softly.

The woman took a moment to respond but eventually gave a small nod of her head and turned her face partly toward him.

'I called yesterday,' he continued, 'and spoke to one of the nursing staff. My name is Leighton Jones; I was wondering if I could talk to you about your daughter.'

The elderly woman sighed. The sound seemed to come from a dark depth within her.

'I have told the papers everything. Why can't you people leave me alone,' she said, and turned away from Leighton.

'I'm not from any paper or magazine,' he said, sitting in a nearby plastic chair. 'I'm a police officer from Oceanside.'

There was a pause in Mrs Cooper's breathing, as if she had taken a quick breath before she spoke. 'If that's true then you're a long way from home.'

'It is true, and I am, but that's how important this situation is,' Leighton said gravely.

'So, what is it that you want from me?' she asked.

'To ask you about Michael Stanton.'

For several moments, Mrs Cooper said nothing at all. The only sound in the room came from a large air conditioning unit that was mounted on the ceiling. As the silence between Leighton and Mrs Cooper expanded, the drone of the machine seemed to swell to a deafening level. Despite the fact he was a patient man,

Leighton was almost ready to leave after five minutes of silence, but that was when Mrs Cooper finally spoke.

'Why do you need to speak to me, has he done it again? I knew it was only a matter of time.'

'Done what again?' Leighton asked.

Mrs Cooper gave a small dismissive shrug.

'Murdered somebody, I suppose – destroyed another family, like he did mine.'

'The records say Stanton was found guilty of involuntary manslaughter, which suggest that the jury believed he never intended to kill anyone. I take it you don't believe that?'

'That was a pathetic story that the defence lawyer came up with to save Stanton from the death penalty he deserved.'

'He started the fire in the lumber store, rather than the house; is it possible that it could have been an accident?'

'Look at me, Detective,' she said, turning toward Leighton. The fire had roasted one half of her face entirely. The skin on her left side looked like pale melted wax, her ear was missing, and her eye was an opaque ball. 'This is what Michael Stanton did to me. He took away my only child and my husband, and broke my heart, body, and mind.'

'I'm sorry,' Leighton said sincerely. 'Did anybody figure out his motive?'

Eileen Cooper sighed. 'He was obsessed with my daughter, Veronica – for quite a while it seems. I later discovered that he had been watching her and following her around town, for months, until he finally got to her. The high school counsellor knew, her friends knew, even his parents were aware, but sadly nobody thought it important enough to pass on to us.'

'That's terrible,' Leighton said.

'What makes it worse is that it was my own fault.' As she spoke, Eileen Cooper began to weep, but only from her functioning eye. Leighton guessed that the tear duct had been fused closed on her other one.

'What do you mean, it was your fault? How?'

'I let that creature into our house that day – I invited him.'

'Can you tell me what happened that day?'

'I could, but I'd rather not. If you want to rake over the past, I'm sure the details are all there in the court records, as well as a few of the less principled crime magazines.'

'Of course.' Leighton nodded. 'I never meant to upset you. I'll leave you in peace. But one last thing: I know this might seem like a strange question, but when they found your daughter, did the medical examiner say anything about her teeth?'

'Mr Jones, by the time the fire crew found my only child, all they had to identify her with were her teeth. If that's what you mean.'

'Thank you,' Leighton said, and stood up. 'I understand how difficult this must be.'

'Do you have any children?' Eileen Cooper asked, with her gaze fixed on Leighton's eyes.

'Yes, a daughter.'

'Living?'

'Yes.'

'Then you can't understand how difficult this is, so don't insult me by claiming to.'

'I'm sorry, Mrs Cooper. It was never my intention to upset you. I'll go now.'

At that moment, something in Leighton's demeanour must have convinced Eileen Cooper that he was worthy of being trusted with at least one piece of private information.

'There *is* something to do with teeth that my daughter said. She told me Stanton had taken something from her drawer.'

'What was it?'

'A small box containing her first tooth. When she was just a little kid, my husband and I told Ronny that the Tooth Fairy never took your first tooth because it was such a special one. Hers was so small and perfect; I can still remember holding it, almost weightless in my hand. That day, after he had been in our house, Ronny told us that Stanton had stolen her baby tooth.' As she spoke, the woman's withered fingers toyed absently with a locket hanging around her wrinkled neck.

'Did you mention the theft to anyone at the time of the fire?'

She shook her head. 'I was in a medically induced coma for seven weeks. When I woke up, my husband and daughter were dead and buried, and my home was ash. All I cared about was seeing the murderer locked up. But I just wanted you to understand what kind of sadistic creature he was.'

'But you got that wish, for a while at least. You know Stanton was released two years ago?'

Eileen Cooper nodded slowly, her eyes fixed on some distant spot. She grimaced as if still unable to accept this fact. 'The son of a bitch only got six years for each member of my family – twelve years for a double murderer.'

'That's only because they said it wasn't a double murder: they said it was accidental.'

'They can say what they like, doesn't make it true. I could see it in that young man's eyes: he was all smiles, but there was nothing in his eyes but hatred. Shakespeare wrote "that one may smile, and smile, and be a villain". Did you know that?'

'No, I didn't, but it does ring true in my own experience.'

'I remember finding out that he had returned here after he was released. I felt like I'd been stabbed.' She rubbed absently at her hands as she spoke.

'Do you worry that he would come to the care home?'

'If I ever see him, I'll shove a fork in his eye and twist it – I keep one with me at all times, just in case. I may look old and frail, but I have the strength to do it.'

'Why do you think he came back?'

'To hide maybe. I don't know. He came back to the town and even got a job mopping floors down at the Sanderson Clinic in town for a while. Of course, that was only until he was recognised and then word got around.'

'What happened after that?'

Eileen Cooper shrugged. 'I heard that after his father died, Stanton sold the family house and moved on, thankfully. I guess if you're here to speak about him, you probably know where he ended up.'

'Yes, I believe I do. Thank you for your time, Mrs Cooper,' Leighton said with a genuinely affectionate smile. He stood up. 'I know that dredging up the past can't be easy for you.'

'Look at me, Mr Jones.' She held up a shiny and misshaped hand, upon which all of the fingers were shrivelled. 'My burns will never heal – on the outside or the inside. My past is with me every damned minute of the day.'

'I'm still sorry,' Leighton said sincerely, and he turned around.

He was almost at the door of the room, several feet away from Mrs Cooper, when she called one last thing to him.

'Mr Jones, if you do get the chance to encounter Michael Stanton, please promise me one thing …'

'Sure.'

'Promise that you will tread carefully. He's a very disturbed man.'

'I will,' Leighton said, and then he left.

After he had gone, Mrs Cooper gazed out of the tall window, toward the gardens. Her face, usually contorted in pain, or lost in the sadness of untouchable memories, looked different today. Today she looked afraid.

The nursing assistant who had initially met Leighton, was sitting waiting for him in the cool corridor that lead to the reception. She was perched on a plain wooden bench, holding a thick ledger in her hands, and smiling self-consciously.

'Mr Jones, before you go, can I ask you to sign this please? I forgot to ask you to complete it when you first arrived. We have to keep an accurate record – in case of any emergency.'

'Of course,' Leighton said. 'Did you get in hot water with someone?' he asked, as he sat down next to her and carefully lifted the book from her hands.

'The home manager, Mr Rankin, likes to ensure that things are always done properly.' When she said the word properly, the nurse rolled her eyes. 'He likes to follow the staff around the place to make sure we are doing everything correct. The thing is, if he makes us leave a job to go back and do another one *properly*, which just keeps the situation going.'

'I honestly feel your pain,' Leighton chuckled. 'I have a boss quite like that myself, back in Oceanside. Listen, do you have a pen? If not, I have one in my jacket, but it's in the car.'

'Oh, see, I'm such a klutz!' the nurse said as she quickly stood up. 'Give me a second and I'll grab one from the desk.'

'No rush,' Leighton said.

Whilst the nurse was gone, Leighton began flicking absently through the brittle pages of the visitors' book. The information on each page was arranged in six neat columns: date, name of visitor, name of resident, visitor signed in, and visitor signed out. Because all of the other names were unfamiliar to Leighton, he found it easy to flick through the pages scanning for Mrs Cooper. As he looked through page after page, it became obvious to him that the elderly woman hadn't received any visitors for years. And then suddenly, in September 2005, her name appeared. Leighton pressed his finger below her name and slid it along to see the name of her visitor. The name was Michael Stanton.

Leighton felt a momentary release of adrenaline somewhere deep in his abdomen. He went quickly through the earlier pages and discovered that this had been the only visit Eileen Cooper had received from her daughter's killer.

'Here we go.' The nurse had returned and was holding a ballpoint pen out to Leighton.

'Thank you.' He took the pen and filled in his name. Then, standing up, he returned the pen and the book to the nurse.

'That's great,' she said, sounding genuinely relieved. 'I'll show you where the exit is.'

They had only taken a couple of steps along the tiled corridor, when Leighton turned to the nurse.

'Listen, I was just wondering, did anybody see what happened when Michael Stanton came here to see Mrs Cooper?'

The nurse stopped walking and deliberately checked over each shoulder before answering. 'When I first started working here, about three years ago, Mrs Cooper had a regular visit every Wednesday from a man called Dale. Somebody told me that he had once been her daughter's boyfriend. Whenever he was here, the two of them would be locked together in conversation about the past. It was the only time of the week you would see Eileen smile. I suppose they shared their memories.'

'So, what happened?'

'One Wednesday afternoon, Dale never showed up. I wasn't working that day, but my friend Grace said that Eileen had sat in the day room waiting until near midnight, but Dale never called or showed up. And then the next day, *he* shows up.'

'Dale?'

'No, Stanton. The woman had probably hated the guy for nearly two decades, and then he turns up here.'

'What did he want?' Leighton asked.

'It's anyone's guess.' The nurse shrugged her shoulders. 'Forgiveness, maybe?'

'Did he get it?'

'Well it was quite strange. I was on shift that day. At first, she was shouting and freaking out, but he said something to her and she just stopped. I had run through from reception, but by the time I got there she just waved me away. He was sitting next to her wearing his thick glasses and a Lakers cap.'

'Could he have threatened her?'

'Possibly, but she was wearing an alarm and the day room was full of visitors. It just doesn't seem likely.'

'Did you call the cops?'

'For what? He served his time; he was just a guy visiting the care home.'

'How long did Stanton spend here?'

'He didn't stay very long, ten, fifteen minutes maybe, and then he left.'

'What about the other guy, I think you called him Dale, when did he show again?'

'He didn't. Not after that, ever. I guess word must have reached him that Eileen had spent the afternoon with the guy who killed his girlfriend. He never came back after that. I sometimes think that's why she sits in the day room from dawn till dusk. I think she's waiting for Dale Sanderson to come back and forgive her.'

'Lonely life,' Leighton said, and walked to the exit of the care home. Part of him noted that his own life wasn't much better. 'Thanks for allowing me to visit,' he said as he left.

35

He had been working on his creation for almost two hours, but finally it was finished. As soon as he was done, he walked into the bathroom, took off his glasses, and stared at his reflection in the mirror. The small box he held in his hand no longer contained his prize; it held new contents.

When he had finished admiring himself, he opened the medicine cabinet, placed the box on the shelf, and closed it once more.

36

Leighton drove his car beneath the ornamental palms of the Golden Cross Care Home's therapeutic gardens and turned onto the dusty main road into town. The town of Lakehead had once been a trading post. It still looked like a frontier town, though the saloons and barber shops had been replaced. Now the town was little more than three parallel streets of glazed shop fronts, and most of those were selling cut-price fashion goods, or local arts and crafts.

As Leighton navigated his way through the small town, he glanced around. Driving down the last street, he eventually found what he had been searching for.

The squat, red brick building was single-storey and had its own small parking lot. It reminded Leighton of a Wild West jailhouse, and he half expected to see barred windows on the side, with the arms of a condemned prisoner stretching out of them toward freedom. Leighton pulled his car into a space and climbed out. The surface of the parking lot was not yet completely unusable, but cracks were beginning to spread across it like veins, and Leighton guessed that by the following summer it would be covered in weeds. A white plastic sign, which hung above the double glass doors of the building, said Sanderson Clinic. The brittle plastic of the sign had been exposed to years of scorching sunlight, and consequently a large crack had split the first word almost in two. Leighton wondered absently how much longer the sign had, before it snapped completely. He avoided the broken sign as he approached the building. Unfortunately, both the doors, and the two large windows, had been smeared white to indicate it was no longer in use.

After attempting unsuccessfully to peer through the opaque glass, Leighton walked around to the rear of the building. Here he discovered nothing more than a square of parched ground, which held nothing more than a large, red, industrial bin. It was red and rectangular like the building. Leighton approached the metal container and paused for a moment before bringing his hand to the black rubber lid.

Although Lisa in dispatch had only been half-joking about Leighton's instinct, he sensed death here and he hesitated for a moment. Eventually, the feeling subsided and, having taken a deep breath, he threw the lid open. He found himself looking at a naked torso and some misshapen limbs. He shuddered, before realising that the flesh was in fact plastic.

It was then that his cell phone rang, and Leighton let the lid drop down on the grim discovery.

He pulled the phone from his pocket and held it to his face.

'Hello?'

'It's me.'

'Annie?'

'No, Rochelle. Listen, I know you'll think I've gone nuts, but Danielle is missing.'

'What?'

'Nobody's seen her for a couple of days; I asked the girls who work the same corners as her. It's like she just vanished overnight. It's just like Jenna, you know?'

Leighton momentarily considered telling Rochelle about Jenna, but he didn't want to add to her woes. He also made a mental association with the phrase "vanished overnight" and what the nurse had said about Dale Sanderson. Maybe the killer didn't only target females.

'Okay, listen to me. I'm up in Lakehead, but if anything happens, you go to the cops, and if you don't feel safe doing that then go to anybody you trust.'

'I'm not freaking out or anything,' Rochelle said unconvincingly. 'It's just not like her. She might be fine. I'm just a bit worried.'

'I'll be down in a couple of hours,' Leighton said softly. 'I promise I'll call you then. Okay?'

'Okay, but I'm going to crash for an hour or two so let it ring a while,' Rochelle said, and hung up.

Leaving his car in the lot of the clinic, Leighton wandered along the main street. The town of Lakehead seemed cosy, almost cheerful. Although it was only a couple of hours drive from the city, it seemed like another country. There were fewer big names out here and none of the warehouse size depot stores. Even the air was different – it smelled heavier than the fresh breezes of Oceanside – but Leighton liked it. This was the kind of place Leighton had often taken Annie to, on their Sunday drives, ten years earlier. Those were golden days; they would sing loudly in the car and stop for ice cream and laugh at silly things. For a moment, Leighton wished he could step into the past. He wondered if Annie would still like places like this. Probably not.

After he'd peered through all the shop windows, Leighton stopped at a small independent coffee shop. The place felt both homely and familiar – a place where bad things couldn't happen. But the experience of the Cooper family suggested quite clearly that they could.

As he stepped into the coffee shop a small bell clanged above the door, and Leighton found he was the only customer in the place.

'Hi there,' said a cheerful woman. She was wearing a chocolate coloured uniform and was carrying a tray of mugs as she moved behind the marble counter.

'Hey,' Leighton smiled, and glanced around the empty tables. 'You having a quiet day?'

'Yeah, not bad, we usually get a dip after breakfast, but I need it to get the place cleaned up for lunch.' As the woman spoke she put down the tray and smoothed her skirt. 'I'm Leanne. What can I get you?'

'Black coffee, please.' Leighton eased himself onto a bar stool at the counter.

'Sure thing,' Leanne said cheerfully, and got busy with the large gleaming machine behind her.

As it cranked and hissed like a mechanical dragon, Leighton looked out of the large window to the bright street outside.

'Leanne, do you know a place here called the Sanderson Clinic?'

'I sure do, though I think you might be a little young for that place. In any case, it's shut down. Here's your coffee.' She placed a coffee cup and saucer on the counter with a small gingerbread man biscuit on the side.

'Thanks,' Leighton said as he snapped one arm off the biscuit and popped it in his mouth. 'What kind of business did it do?'

'The clinic? It supplied all sorts of care items for the elderly: walking aids, bath hoists, wheel chairs, all that kind of stuff.' Leanne checked off each item on her fingers, as if she were reciting a food order. 'My Aunt Lara is bothered with arthritis and used to get her knee braces from there. Now she has to get my uncle to drive her down to Escondido every six months for them.'

'Did any of the clinic's employees ever come in here?'

'Yeah, some of them.'

'I'm interested in a guy who used to work there, can you remember any of them?'

'Sure, you from Border Control?' Leanne raised her eyebrows suspiciously.

'No,' Leighton smiled. 'Oceanside Police – though I don't know if that's better or worse.'

'You got any ID?'

'Sure.' Leighton produced his badge from his trouser pocket.

'Looks reasonably convincing,' Leanne said, nodding her head. 'Who you interested in?'

'Michael Stanton?' Leighton said.

'Shit, has he done it again?'

'You're the second person today who responded like that when I said his name.'

'Who was the other one?' Leanne asked.

'Eileen Cooper,' Leighton replied.

'That poor woman,' Leanne said, her eyes softening. 'He destroyed her. In some ways, I think it may have been better if she had died too.'

'She told me that she blames herself for her daughter's death. Do you know what she means?'

'Well, my kid sister was friends with Ronny Cooper – Veronica – in high school. Back then Ronny had just started dating Dale Sanderson, but her parents hadn't met him or anything. Dale was the nicest guy and a real athlete too, he swam for the school team, and Ronny would watch him train most nights – checking out all those muscles. I think it was just the young love stage, when the rest of the world doesn't matter a damn. You know what I mean?'

'Yeah, the best days,' Leighton said with a melancholy smile. He chuckled into his coffee cup.

'Anyway, Ella – my kid sister – told me that on the day of the fire, Ronny had called up a couple of her girlfriends to say that some creep from her history class had stalked her to her house. Apparently, he had showed up on her front porch, all bashful smiles, with his glasses on and his hair combed down. Eileen was painting the hallway when he'd come to the door and told her that he was a friend of her daughter's. She naturally thought that he must be the boy her daughter had been spending every hour with, so she invited him in.'

'Thinking he was Dale?' Leighton asked.

'Yeah exactly. But the thing is, because the house was all covered in wet paint, she told the guy to go on up and wait in Veronica's room.'

'Where was Veronica, at home?'

'No, she had come down into town, to the general store, to pick up some taco shells for dinner.'

'How far away is their house from town?' Leighton asked.

'You mean how far away *was* their house? It's nothing but a piece of black dirt now, but it's only five minutes out of town, on the western side.'

'So, did Veronica come home to discover a stranger in her bedroom?'

'Yeah, and that's when the shit really hit the fan. Apparently, when Ronny showed up, Stanton told her that he had loved her since junior high and they should be together. He even got down on his knees and pulled out a wedding ring for her.'

'What happened, did they call the cops?' Leighton asked.

'They didn't need to. Ronny was screaming and her dad, Steven Cooper, who had his own lumber yard next to the house, heard and ran into the house. Ronny said her dad dragged Stanton out of their home and threw him into the street. Anyway, that was when she'd called round her friends to warn them about the psycho. But she didn't need to do that.'

'What do you mean?' Leighton asked.

'He was only ever interested in one girl: Veronica Cooper. A few hours after Michael Stanton was thrown out of the Cooper family home, he showed up again during the night. He was drunk and angry, so he torched the place. Ronny and her dad died in the fire. Some people say he died trying to get to his daughter, but I don't know if that's just a rumour. Anyhow, I guess Eileen believes that because she let the psycho into their house, she's to blame.'

'It's not her fault,' Leighton said definitively. 'He would have just been rejected another time, and the outcome would most likely have been the same.'

'Yeah, I can see that, but I guess guilt can stop a person from thinking clearly.'

'Mrs Cooper told me that Stanton returned here after he'd served his time in jail, is that right?'

Leanne nodded. 'He showed up here a couple of weeks after he was released. Found himself a job in the clinic, here in town. All the businesses in town got a yellow letter from the parole office, asking if we would be willing to help the guy fit back into society.'

'Were you?'

'Hell no! I reckon the clinic was the only place that said yes.' Leanne shrugged. 'So that's where he ended up. He mopped floors there.'

'For how long?'

'Not long, three or four months maybe. I guess after his dad died, and he sold the house, he didn't need to grub around for money anymore.'

'When did the place close down?' Leighton asked.

'Around the same time as he left. I reckon Dale Sanderson decided he deserved something more, or maybe having Stanton resurface had brought it all back again.'

'Dale? You mean he worked in the clinic where Stanton ended up?'

'Oh yes, he owned the place, that was the only reason Stanton got the job. Dale told us all that Stanton had served his time and deserved another shot. He said it was what Veronica would have wanted. But I'm not so sure she would have. The place has been sitting empty for more than a year now. It might be like that for years to come. Nothing happens quickly around here.'

At that moment, a group of giggling teenagers came through the door, and soaked up Leanne's attention with orders of iced lattes and grilled sandwiches. Leighton slipped a couple of tens under his coffee cup.

'Thank you,' he called across the counter, 'for both the coffee and your time.'

'Any time,' Leanne said, as she cut some sub rolls. 'You take care.'

When Leighton climbed back into his car, he saw that his cell phone screen was illuminated with a message indicating that he had two missed calls. Picking up the handset, he dialled his voicemail and held it to his ear. An automated voice told him the time of the first message then Annie's voice followed it:

'Hey, Dad, it's me. I got your message and I'm still at Lina's place, but don't worry about it, I should be home tomorrow night. Okay, hope you're catching bad guys. Later.'

There was a click, and the automated voice returned to announce the second message:

'Jonesy, it's Danny. Listen, don't freak out, okay. I just thought you should know that Gretsch fired me. He somehow got word of where I was, and he called the hospital to check. Somebody at reception confirmed that I'd been here most of the week. He called me on my cell phone, told me to come in next week to go through dismissal procedures.'

Leighton removed the phone from his ear and looked at it as if it had just burned him.

37

It was just after 6pm. and Gretsch was in the parking lot, climbing on his gleaming Harley, when Leighton Jones drove into the car park and screeched to a halt in front of him. He sighed as Leighton hurried out of the vehicle, leaving the door hanging open. The captain had been expecting this confrontation and was well prepared for it.

'What do you want, Jones?' Gretsch asked as he straddled his bike and folded his arms across his chest.

'I just spoke with Danny,' Leighton shouted. 'You fired him? Jesus Christ, are you serious?'

'Don't try to lay this shit on me,' Gretsch said with a fixed grin. 'If you're looking for someone to blame, try looking in the mirror. This is all your mess, Jones.'

'Mine? How the hell do you figure that?' Leighton narrowed his eyes to slits.

'You were the senior officer, Danny has barely got five years under his belt. What the hell were you thinking?'

'I was *thinking* that a loyal officer's father is dying, and maybe he should be with him. Danny is entitled to be with his family.'

'That's not your call to make – thankfully!'

'Is that what this is about, your bruised ego? You being the boss is all that matters!'

'He's been fired, Jones, get over it.'

Leighton shook his head in disbelief. 'Danny's old man didn't have insurance. He was fire crew – one of our own.'

'So?' Gretch's face remained impassive.

'The family are having to cover the costs of his medical treatment alone. If Danny has no income, it falls to his sister. Is that what you want, to destroy a family?'

'My heart bleeds, Jones, it really does. Maybe you should've considered that before you allowed – no – *enabled* another officer to put himself in dereliction of duty.'

'There was no "dereliction of duty"; I was there covering all the shifts, and both the driver classes were taught.'

'Protocols were ignored.' Gretsch said the words with real gravitas.

'Ah,' Leighton smiled bitterly. 'The all-important protocols. Well, I'm glad that you now feel in control again. Sleep easy, Captain.'

Leighton turned and walked angrily back to his car.

'Oh, and before you go,' Gretsch called.

'What?' Leighton asked without turning around.

'You're suspended for three weeks. You deliberately filed false reports stating Officer Clark was with you.'

Leighton looked back over his shoulder at the captain.

'So, you fire Danny for neglecting his duties then you force me to neglect my duties? That makes strategic sense!'

'I think you don't need me to fuck up your policing.'

'So, when another body shows up, or another girl gets abducted, you'll be happy enough to explain your decision to the media?'

'That's not going to happen though, is it? And the reason it's not going to happen, is because the real homicide detectives have the suspect in custody. His DNA was found on her body. That means you can get back to logging DUIs and leave the real police work to us.'

'And you can't figure out how a known rapist's DNA might end up on a warm, naked body that was dumped on his known route to work? Yeah that's a real tough one Captain.'

'The case is closed,' Gretsch said.' You go anywhere near this investigation and you'll be looking for a new job alongside your buddy.'

'You're making a big mistake, Captain. The killer is here in Oceanside. He has already served time for a double murder over in … I have a name, Michael Stanton – he's a potential suspect, and I have credible evidence that justifies further investigation.'

'Who?' Gretsch held up a hand to his ear, and for a moment Leighton thought he might actually be interested.

'Michael Stanton, he killed a father and daughter in a house fire back in 1988.'

'Sounds like bullshit to me. Go home, Jones. You've got nada. And hand in your gun and your badge at reception.' Gretsch straddled his bike, started the engine, and revved out of the station parking lot.

Leighton climbed into his car, slammed the door, and drove straight into the captain's designated parking space. Having switched off the engine, he hurried into the building and downstairs to the driver records department. If nobody else was going to do anything to stop this psycho, he sure as hell would.

38

Ryan Slater switched off his car engine and reached into his shirt pocket. The piece of paper he pulled out had been folded twice into a neat white square. It felt strange to be out in the field without his partner, Goza, but this trip was strictly off the record. Gretsch had called him from his cell phone and given him the name of some poor ex-con that Leighton Jones imagined was The Dentist. The captain had asked Slater to use his detective skills to get an address, so he could go and warn the poor guy that a loony traffic cop was gunning for him. Slater was, of course, more than happy to oblige. In his opinion, guys like Jones were dinosaurs who had no place in modern policing. The days of crossing boundaries and pursuing hunches were long gone. If Slater could do anything to help nudge Leighton Jones out of Oceanside PD, he would willingly oblige.

After Gretsch had hung up, Slater got busy putting together a list of all the residents named Michael Stanton living in the area. There was only one with a prior conviction and Slater had tracked him down to a house in a residential street on the east side of the city. He decided to use his own car for the trip, that way he would remain off the radar.

After a half hour drive from the station, he found himself in a quiet residential area, where he parked his car and checked the details once more.

Slater pressed the doorbell and, while he waited, adjusted his tie for maximum professionalism. After a moment the door was opened by a clean-shaven man wearing frameless glasses.

'Can I help you?' he asked, from behind the door, which was only partially open.

'Mr Stanton?'

'Yes,' the man said, with a small nod of his head.

'My name is Detective Slater. Could I come in and speak to you for a moment?'

'What's it about?' Stanton asked, whilst running a hand absently through his neat hair.

'It's a rather delicate matter,' Slater said quietly. 'I'd just as soon speak to you inside.'

'Of course,' Stanton said, as he stepped aside and welcomed Slater through the doorway.

Stanton closed the door and led the detective into a tidy living area at the rear of the property. The walls of the room were white, and a large patio window looked out onto a small barbecue area. If Slater was ever asked to describe Stanton's home, he would probably use the word 'clinical'.

'Please, take a seat,' Stanton said with a broad smile. 'It's so hot today. Would you like some lemonade?'

'Sure,' Slater said as he sat down, 'that would be great.'

A moment later, Stanton returned with two glasses of cloudy lemonade and chiming ice cubes. He handed one glass to Slater and, keeping hold of the other, he carefully sat down on a nearby chair.

'Nice place you got here,' Slater said.

'It's small but it suits me just fine. So, what's bothering you, Officer … Slater, wasn't it?'

Slater nodded, took a drink, and wiped his mouth with the back of his hand.

'Well, it's a bit embarrassing, I guess. There's a traffic cop at the station who is a joke – imagines himself as a frustrated detective; in reality he's a loony. Anyway, he's got it into his head that you're a deranged killer.'

'Me?' Stanton laughed. 'A killer of house plants maybe.'

'Yeah, well that's pretty much why my boss wanted me to give you a heads-up, just in case this guy shows up looking to ask you anything. His name is Leighton Jones and he works traffic.'

Obviously, you don't have to speak to him. Just call Oceanside PD and we'll come and get him.'

'That's very kind of you,' Stanton said with a genuine smile.

'No problem,' Slater said, and took a large drink.

'Have you, or your boss, any idea why this Jones guy would zero in on me in particular?'

'No.' Slater shrugged. 'He's full of oddball ideas. The guy got lucky on a missing person case a few years back, so now he thinks he's Sherlock fucking Holmes. Apparently, he said something about a similar crime in Lakehead, where you have a prior conviction for fire-raising.'

Slater noted a flicker of something appear, then vanish again, in Stanton's expression.

'But that was twenty years ago, I was a dumb kid who had a fascination with fire. I stupidly torched a lumber barn for the hell of it. Unfortunately, the fire spread to a nearby house. A couple of people died because of my stupidity.' He shook his head slowly. 'I fucked up and I spent sixteen years in a state penitentiary for my mistake. I know what I am. It hardly makes me Ted Bundy.'

'Exactly.' Slater shrugged. 'But this guy is like Columbo – he sees suspects in every alleyway.'

'So, who else knows about this guy's wild theories then?'

'Just the three of us, 'Slater said, ' the captain, Jones, and me. That's all.'

'Thank God! For a moment, I was thinking I'd have half of Oceanside PD hunting me down, like O.J Simpson!' He let out a nervous laugh.

'No, you're quite safe,' Slater said with a smile. 'This guy's ideas are out there. Nobody gives a shit about his whacko theories.'

'That's great,' Stanton said with a genuine sigh of relief, 'you've really helped me out, Officer.'

'Detective,' Slater corrected.

'Sorry, Detective. Here, can I get you a refill?'

Slater drained the contents of his glass and handed it to Stanton, who walked into the kitchen.

There was a large mirror on one wall of the room in which Slater sat. It was angled in such a way that, if he leaned back a little, Slater could see a small area of the bright green kitchen. As he glanced in the mirror, he could see that Stanton was just standing there, holding the two glasses in his hands. He wasn't attempting to refill them at all; he was simply standing, staring into space, as if waiting for something. Slater thought he had perhaps forgotten what he was doing.

'So, what is it you do here in Oceanside, Mr Stanton?' he asked, hoping to remind the guy that his visitor was still here.

'Well,' Stanton called through, 'mainly I kill hookers.'

Slater laughed so much that he made himself cough. Then he couldn't stop coughing, and when he tried to bring his hand up to his throat, he found that his arm would not work.

At that point, Stanton walked back into the room. 'Ah good,' he said in a quiet voice, 'the arsenic is working quite nicely. We'll get you into the trunk of my car very soon. But in the meantime, you just sit there and relax.'

39

Nina Shindel had just lifted a paper bag of groceries out of her sports car, and closed the trunk, when she noticed her visitor sitting on the stone doorstep of her small, single-story home.

'Hey there, Officer,' she called to Leighton as she walked over to her front door. 'We've really got to stop meeting like this.'

'Ah, you're home.' Leighton smiled and stood up. 'Look, I'm really sorry to bother you at home, Nina, but it seems like I'm on the blacklist down at the medical examiner's HQ.'

'It certainly looks that way,' Nina said with a smile. 'Can I make you a coffee?'

'No, thank you,' Leighton said graciously. 'I wouldn't want you to get in trouble for fraternising with the enemy.'

'It's fine, I'm not a fan of being told who I can and cannot speak to. In any case, it would be less obvious to step inside than stand talking out here in the open.'

'Okay then,' Leighton conceded, 'a black coffee would be great.'

Nina led Leighton through the front door into a white house, which was stylish and wonderfully cool inside.

'It feels great in here,' Leighton said as he took a seat at the breakfast bar.

'I have the air conditioner on a timer, it kicks in half an hour before I get home – if I manage to get home on time.' Nina filled the kettle and switched it on.

'You been here long?' Leighton asked.

'Three years now. I used to stay in a bigger place, near the coast, but I got divorced and once I'd untangled myself out of that situation, I decided I would rather have somewhere small, but all mine.'

'I get that,' Leighton said.

The kettle reached a rumbling climax and Nina filled a cafetière, which sat between her and Leighton like an old-style TNT detonator.

'What is it you want to know?' Nina asked, as she pulled two mugs from a cupboard.

'The girl that I came to see you about, the one with the flame tattoo on her neck, well I think they have arrested the wrong person for her murder,'

Nina paused and looked directly at Leighton. 'Go on,' she said.

'And I believe that maybe the killer is still out there… picking up more victims.'

'Okay, you have your theory, so what do you want from me?' Nina pushed the plunger down on the coffee and divided the steaming liquid between the two mugs.

'Well, I heard there was another body found, out at Lake Tanner, Jenna Dodds.'

'Yeah, I know the one. The body was brought in on Tuesday afternoon. And I suppose you want to know if the two females could have been killed by the same person?'

'Could they have?' Leighton raised his eyebrows.

'Yes.' Nina shrugged 'But in reality, that doesn't mean an awful lot, other than it is a possibility.'

'It's unlikely then?'

'I didn't say that. Look, I'll tell you what I know. Partly because I like you, but mostly because I'm not convinced that your colleagues are too interested in pursuing this case. From my examination, both females were murdered. Jenna Dodds was already dead when she went into the lake. But that's not the best – or worst – part, from your point of view. There is another, more significant connection between the two.'

'What do you mean?'

'Both of the bodies I examined were missing a tooth. Now that's not always surprising, especially if a victim has been assaulted, but both of these victims lost a lower front tooth around the same time of their deaths; I even noted this detail in my reports.'

'You mean the victims had both been punched?'

'No,' Nina said, shaking her head.

'What then?' Leighton asked.

'They'd been intentionally extracted.'

'Oh.' Leighton sipped his coffee. 'How do you know?'

Nina rolled her eyes. 'I know because I have been doing this job for more than a couple of weeks.'

'Sorry,' Leighton offered.

Nina sighed. 'If a person is punched in the face, hard enough to knock a tooth out, there are other injuries: one or both lips would show signs of trauma, inside and out. There were no abrasions on the inside of the mouth, on either of the bodies I examined. No other teeth on either side of the missing one were loose either. There was, however, some mandibular bruising, where the victims jaw was gripped, presumably when the tooth was removed. This was no crude removal with a big pair of pliers either. Whoever took these trophies was careful about it.'

'Jeez,' Leighton said as he shifted on his stool. 'So, he's deliberately pulled a tooth from each of the victims; was this some type of torture?'

'No,' Nina said, and took a sip of coffee. 'The procedure was carried out post-mortem in both cases. And I also heard this morning that the media have already got hold of this detail – most likely bribed somebody in Homicide for it – and they're calling the killer The Dentist. Hardly a surprise.'

'Shit. Media attention won't help,' Leighton frowned.

'No,' Nina agreed. 'Once he has a national audience, the killer will have to up his game and live up to his celebrity reputation. Do you know about the third girl?' she asked.

'What?' Leighton felt his stomach tighten.

'I thought you would have heard at the station?'

'No.' Leighton shook his head. 'I'm on compulsory leave. What happened?'

'A third body was brought in first thing this morning. She had been dumped at the back of a vacant lot on North River Road.'

'Shit, was she also missing a tooth?'

'I couldn't honestly tell you; I didn't examine her – they've moved me up to the soft tissue lab. But I did see her getting brought in, and you know what the weird thing was?'

'What?'

'Physically, she looked just like the others: same height, same hair colour – not all the same age, but close enough to pass for each other. So, whilst I couldn't say for certain, I would say it's a fair bet that the third girl will be missing a tooth too.'

Leighton realised with horror that the situation was making increasingly horrible sense.

'Look, thanks for this, Nina. I know you're taking a chance speaking to me,' Leighton said with a smile.

'Any time.' Nina smiled. 'Just don't tell anyone in official circles that you were here.'

'My lips are sealed,' he said, and left Nina to put away her groceries.

40

Danny was using a damp flannel to mop his sleeping father's forehead, when Leighton gently knocked on the frame of the open door. The room was small and too warm. The sweeping fan on the bedside table was doing little to lower the temperature.

'Hi, partner, mind if I join the party?' Leighton asked quietly.

'Hey, Jonesy,' Danny said softly, 'of course, in you come. Grab a seat. I'm just trying to keep my papa cool. This place always feels like a pizza oven. They say it's to keep him comfortable, but I reckon it's to keep the patients half asleep. Makes life easier for the staff I guess.'

Leighton stepped gingerly into the white room and sat in a leather seat at the foot of the bed. Danny's father was sleeping: a small oxygen mask was attached to his face.

'I take it you got my message about the captain, huh?' Danny asked.

'Yeah,' Leighton nodded. 'I'm sorry, Danny, this is all my fault. I spoke to Gretsch this afternoon, but he was in asshole mode – well, even more than usual.'

'It's okay, Jonesy,' Danny smiled. 'I pretty much knew the risks in coming up here. To be honest, this is where I should be. When he showed up here, this morning, I honestly didn't care. He wanted to enjoy the moment of actually firing me – to see the shock in my face. In reality, I was just too tired to give a shit.' Danny took his father's hand as he spoke. 'I don't know if he'll pull through, I just know I should be here with him. You were right about that.'

'Even if I was, it's still not right that you get in trouble; I'll do whatever I can to fix it, you have my word.' Leighton looked tired but determined.

'It's cool, Jonesy. I'll find something else, hopefully. Right now, my priority is to be here with this old guy. Anyway, what have you been up to? Did you manage to dig up anything in Lakehead?'

'Yeah, I did.' Leighton sighed and sat back in the chair. 'I reckon I've maybe got him, Danny. I might just know who the sonofabitch is.'

'What you gonna do?' Danny placed the flannel down on the bedside table and sat on the edge of the bed.

'I took what I'd found to Slater and Gretsch, but neither of them gives a shit. I'm thinking about following up the lead myself.'

'What about the day job?' Danny asked. 'You know how Gretsch will act if he catches you moonlighting.'

'That won't be a problem, Gretsch has already suspended me.'

'Jeez, Jonesy. Why did he do that – is it because you covered for me?'

'Look, you know Gretsch, he would have found a reason to punish me regardless of anything we did.'

Danny slowly shook his head in disbelief. 'I'm sorry, Jonesy. Man, I know this will end up on your record.'

'Don't worry about it. I was never destined to have a clean service record.'

'So, what's your big plan?'

'I'm going to visit the suspect's last known address. There was only his registered address in Lakehead in the system, but I looked up the parole records, and it turns out that Michael Stanton has relocated here, in the city. If there's anything in his home connecting him to the abductions, we could possibly get him.'

'You sure that's a good idea? If you're right, then this prick is dangerous.'

'Take a look at my life, Danny. I've got nothing to lose. Some young rookie, with a wife and a couple of kids, could eventually get sent in and end up dead.'

'Everyone has something to lose, Jonesy. Why don't you wait a couple of days? My sister will be back down from Vegas and then I could come with you.'

'I've already dragged you into enough trouble. Look, I'm a careful old bastard. I'll drop by the address and read the situation. If it looks hot, I'll get out of there.'

'You promise?'

Leighton stood up and saw that Danny's expression showed fear. The guy was on the brink of losing his father, and he'd suddenly realised that everybody was vulnerable to mortality.

'I'll be careful, Danny, I swear.'

'I hope so, Jonesy.' Danny stood up and squeezed Leighton's hand. 'Thanks for coming over, man.'

'Don't worry about it, Danny. And I'll fix the work thing, maybe speak to the chief. Either way, you'll be okay.'

On his way home from the hospital, Leighton swung his car down to the Boulevard, which ran like a spine through the city. The sun had slipped behind the horizon and the canopy of sky over Oceanside was fading from orange through to violet. Leighton tapped his fingers anxiously on the steering wheel for a moment, before taking out his cell phone and dialling Annie's number. It rang for a moment then connected.

'Hey, Annie, it's dad, I—'

An automated voice interrupted him, telling him he had reached his daughter's voicemail and to leave a message after the tone. Leighton waited patiently before speaking again.

'Hi, Annie, it's dad, I was hoping that—' without warning the call ended. Leighton shook his head and dialled the number again. This time, the automated voice told him that the phone he was calling was switched off. After staring out through the windshield for a moment, Leighton scrolled through his contacts until he found Lena Dupree's number.

'Hi, Lina, this is Annie's dad. Do you know where she is?'

'Yes, Mr Jones. Annie's with me.'

'Ah great, can I speak to her?'

'No.'

'No?'

'She says she doesn't want to speak to you right now.'

'What?'

'She tried phoning you about twenty times today just to meet for lunch.'

'Tell her I'm really sorry, I was caught up with some police business.'

There was a mumble in the background as Lina relayed his message.

'Look, it's always the same with you: you're never around, and when you are you just criticise her.'

'That's crazy. I only tell her she needs to get a job.'

'Exactly.'

'Please just let me speak to her.'

'Goodbye, Mr Jones,' Lina said, and hung up.

Leighton dragged a hand over his face and groaned in frustration. He felt torn between two equally vulnerable people, except Rochelle had fewer options than Annie.

At various points throughout the day, Leighton's thoughts had returned to Rochelle. It seemed that her instincts had been correct all along. More alarming was the fact that the victims had all looked alike. Leighton realised there were a limited number of girls working the streets of Oceanside, and Rochelle was one who matched the killer's type. Regardless of his own course of action, he now needed to ensure that she was safe. He checked the time, it was 9.15pm. He figured it could be early enough for Rochelle to be at work.

Eventually he spotted Rochelle beneath the hard glare of a streetlight. She was sitting on a bench, smoking a cigarette, watching the passing cars with a jaded interest.

He honked his horn and Rochelle looked up, frowned, and then grinned. Leighton was surprised that she looked genuinely pleased to see him as she hurried over to where he had parked up.

'Hop in,' he called from the window.

'Hey,' she said as she climbed into the car. 'Did you come by earlier?' Her voice was clearly concerned.

'Did I come by here?' Leighton asked.

'No, to my apartment.'

'Not me, I was up in Lakehead until three-ish, and when I got here I stopped off at the hospital. Why?'

'Probably nothing, I crashed out for a while after I called you. But a couple of times I thought I heard somebody rattling the door.'

'Was it locked?' Leighton asked.

'It's always locked.'

'Good. That makes you smarter than most folks. I was wondering if you wanted to grab some food.'

'You know I'm meant to be working, right?' Rochelle raised her eyebrows.

'Well, not on an empty stomach.'

'You don't have to feed me up you know,' Rochelle said defensively. 'I'm doing okay, you know.'

Leighton looked at her for a moment – stick thin, alone in the world, but still fighting to defend her place in it.

'I know that,' Leighton said, nodding his head sincerely. 'I was heading to the drive thru anyway. I figured that, whilst I was there, I could get us both a burrito or something?'

'Well, in that case ...' Rochelle nodded and pulled on her seatbelt.

Having picked up some food from Taco Bell on the Boulevard, Leighton drove toward the harbour.

'So, what's the story with Danielle?' he asked, as the car slid beneath the palm trees and the neon signs.

'Just like I said.' Rochelle shrugged. 'She's off the radar.'

'For how long, a couple of days?'

'Yeah, at least,' Rochelle said.

'When was the last time you saw her?'

'That night when she spoke to you.'

He considered telling Rochelle that he believed both her friends might be lying on a shelf in the medical examiner's office, but he wasn't sure what good it would do. Instead, he shared a small part of the truth.

'Somebody attacked me that same night,' Leighton said.

'Shit. Do you think it was him?'

'I don't know, maybe.' Leighton suddenly looked self-conscious. 'Look, will you do something for me?'

'What?'

'Will you stay off the streets for a couple of days, just till I've had time to check out an address that's come up?'

'Damn, Leighton. This is how I pay for my weekly shopping.'

'I'll buy your shopping for those days you're off the streets,' Leighton said.

'After tonight, you mean?'

'No.' He shook his head. 'I mean including tonight.'

'Jeez.' Rochelle looked scared. 'Then you think he got Danielle, don't you? Be fucking straight with me!'

'I don't know for sure, but yes, I think it's possible. Look, I was thinking, if you really did hear somebody at your door, maybe you could stay at my place for a couple of days, or maybe just for tonight?'

Leighton had thought Rochelle would put up an argument, so he was shocked when she simply agreed.

As they arrived at the safety of Leighton's house, both he and Rochelle could hear the shrill sound of the telephone ringing inside. However, by the time Leighton had unlocked his front door and let them in, the caller had rung off.

'Welcome to Jonestown,' Leighton said as he closed the door behind them.

'Not too shabby,' Rochelle said as she gazed at the white walls and large sofas.

'Look around if you want. I'll grab us some plates and something to wash down the food.'

'Don't worry about a plate for me,' Rochelle said, 'I just use the wrapper.'

'Just a beer then?' he offered.

'Sure.'

Leighton vanished into the kitchen and was rummaging in his fridge when he heard a delighted squeal.

'You have a bathtub!' Rochelle sounded impressed.

'What?'

'You've got a tub. I asked the leasing agent if I could have one fitted, but they said it would waste too much water. I couldn't have afforded it anyway.'

'Well, feel free to try it out.' Leighton said as he brought the food through, along with two bottles of beer. 'I only ever use the shower.' He didn't tell her the reason why he hated the white enamel tub.

They sat, side by side, on Leighton's sofa and ate their burritos, using the flattened wrappers for plates.

'Is this a typical Friday night for you?' Rochelle asked.

'I guess.' Leighton shrugged. 'Sometimes I stop in at the Rooster.'

'You're better off here,' Rochelle said, 'but you've got to stop eating junk food.'

'You eat it too,' he said.

'Yeah, well, I don't have a choice,' Rochelle said, 'but if I had a proper job and a nice place with a kitchen, I'd learn to cook nice food.'

'What would that "nice food" be?' Leighton raised his eyebrows.

'I don't know, pasta maybe, with fresh herbs and stuff like that.' Rochelle smiled. 'Oh, and ground black pepper too.'

'Sounds pretty good. Okay.' Leighton nodded. 'I promise I'll get around to cooking properly one day.'

'You better,' she said insistently.

Rochelle sipped her beer and looked at Leighton.

'Thanks for this,' she said quietly.

In that moment, Leighton glimpsed just how vulnerable and frightened Rochelle was. 'It's okay,' he said, 'I just didn't know how else to keep you safe.'

'You don't have to look out for me you know. I've been surviving out there in the world for a long time.'

'Yeah,' Leighton sighed, 'well maybe you deserve better than just survival.' 'Maybe I do,' Rochelle agreed, 'but that doesn't mean anything in the real world. How many people get what they deserve in life – good or bad?'

'Not very many,' Leighton conceded. 'Why don't you just quit; do something else?'

'Yeah, like it's that fucking easy. The only employers looking for women with a history of substance abuse and prostitution are pimps. I have limited employability.'

'Well, maybe one step at a time then.'

'But, I am going to stop – one day.'

'Really?' Leighton asked.

'Yeah, really. I'm going to head to the Midwest, get a little place. I've been saving my money for more than a year.' As she spoke, Rochelle's eyes lit up and she seemed happier than he had ever seen her before.

'The Midwest, huh?' Leighton smiled.

'Seriously,' Rochelle nodded vigorously. 'I've got a nice little place picked out in Oregon.'

'Why there? Is it that *Little House on the Prairie* thing again?'

Rochelle shrugged and blushed a little. 'Yeah, maybe. I don't know, it just seems far enough away to start again. I could be somebody other than just another hooker on the Boulevard.'

'I thought you spent your earnings on drugs. You said you were still using.'

Rochelle shot Leighton a look to check his expression for judgement. Having found none, she explained her situation.

'When Billy dropped off the grid, he left me with no money, a black eye, and a half kilo bag of dust. At first I used that to get off the crack.'

'The lesser of two evils, huh?' Leighton asked.

'I guess. Now I just take a little hit before I go out every night. That way I control my habit and I can keep my nightly earnings to add to my fund.'

'The Oregon fund?'

'Damn right.'

'Sounds like a plan,' Leighton said.

'Hey, hang on, I got an idea.' Rochelle reached across the floor to where her purse was lying. She pulled it onto her lap and rummaged around in it for a moment. She then pulled out two, small yellow cubes.

'Look,' she said as she held them out in her palm.

'What are they?'

'A couple of dice, dices, whatever. I got them out of a Christmas cracker one year, but I held on to them, just to, you know, remind me.'

'Of what?' Leighton asked.

'That it can all change; it can get better with another roll of the dice. It kind of keeps me on the path – even when things are shitty. Here, you should take one of them.'

'What?'

'Well, I only need one, and maybe it'll keep you on the path too.'

'The path to what?' Leighton asked.

'I don't know-cooking good food – for a start.'

The hand held out to Leighton was so generous and sincere that he could not refuse. He took the small yellow cube from Rochelle and dropped into his shirt pocket.

'Thank you, I'll keep it safe,' he said with a warm smile.

'You'd better do. I'll be checking up.'

They ate and drank in silence, but after a while Rochelle saw Leighton looking increasingly distant. It was clear that his thoughts had moved to locating the killer.

'When are you going to this address?' Rochelle asked.

'Tomorrow – in the afternoon,' Leighton said, and took a gulp of beer.

'What's the story with it, do you know something more than you're saying?'

'I think I might have found him, right here in the city.'

'The prick who's doing this shit?'

'Yeah.' Leighton shrugged. 'Maybe. I have a couple of theories.'

'So, are you going to his place with like, a SWAT team or something?'

'No, it'll only be me.'

'What? Why aren't you bringing in all your cop buddies?'

'They won't help me: I'm suspended,' Leighton said apologetically.

'Drunk on duty, I knew those beers at the Rooster were real.' Rochelle winked.

'Nothing like that. They've been desperate to get to me for years.'

'Isn't there anyone else? Couldn't you call the papers or something?'

'I'm not sure that anybody cares about what's happening – not really.'

'Except you, like a badass lone wolf,' Rochelle said with a self-conscious smile.

'I'm just trying to help,' Leighton said quietly.

'Have you got a gun?'

'Yeah, I had to hand in my Glock but I always keep my own pistol and baton handy, so there's no need to worry,' Leighton said, unconvincingly.

'Well, I'll head back to my place tomorrow,' Rochelle shrugged. 'I swear, if I don't hear from you checking in with me, I'm calling anybody who'll listen.'

'You might find that you'll be phoning around for a while,' Leighton said with a wry smile and took another sip of beer.

When Leighton was busy tidying up the kitchen after dinner, Rochelle appeared, sheepishly, in the doorway.

'Would it really be okay if I jumped in that tub?' she asked.

'Sure,' Leighton smiled. 'There are clean towels on the shelf in the corner. You can have the bedroom; I'll have a shave and a shower after you. I'll crash out in Annie's room, so the double is yours. There's no TV in there but the small radio on the shelf works fine if you want some music.'

An hour later, Rochelle was sitting wrapped in a towel on the bottom of Leighton's bed. She was drying her hair, when the absurdity of the situation struck her. She switched off the droning device.

'Hey, Leighton,' she shouted, 'what would your buddies at the station say if they knew you were spending the night with a prostitute?'

'Huh?' he replied from the bathroom.

Standing up, Rochelle, who was still in the towel, walked to the doorway of the bedroom. That was when she found herself confronted by two shocked-looking teenage girls. Annie Jones was standing next to her friend Lina – who appeared to be enjoying the family drama.

'Hey there.' Rochelle smiled and adjusted her robe. 'Your dad invited me.'

'Dad!' Annie screamed.

Leighton came out of the bathroom with a towel tied around his waist and a smear of shaving cream on one cheek.

'You're with a fucking prostitute?' Annie shouted, her voice cracking with emotion.

'Hang on a minute,' Leighton said as he held up a placating hand. 'It's not like that.'

'Yeah, it's clearly all in my mind. There's a hooker in your bedroom and you're almost naked. Do you think I'm that fucking stupid?' Annie looked hurt and angry.

'Hey, watch your mouth,' Leighton said.

'What?' Annie's eyes widened in horror. 'Are you seriously trying to lecture me about good morals?'

'Annie, I'm working on a case – a serious one – and Rochelle is helping me.'

'I'll bet she is,' Lina muttered with a barely concealed snigger.

'Excuse me?' Leighton said, tilting his head to make eye contact with Lina. 'Since when was this any of your business?'

'Maybe since your daughter started spending more time in my house than yours.'

'How could you?' Annie said. 'You're such a liar. All those times you told me your bullshit philosophy about doing the right thing in life.'

'You need to hear me out,' Leighton said, but he knew already that he was wasting his time.

'Come on Lina,' Annie said, 'let's get out of here. My dad's clearly got plans for tonight.'

'Hey,' Rochelle said, 'your dad's telling the truth. He's a good man.'

'What the hell do you know?' Annie snapped.

'More than you, Little Miss Smartass.'

'Fuck you!' Annie said, and grabbed her friend's arm as they stormed out of the house.

As the door slammed, Leighton sat down and dragged his hands over his face.

'I'm sorry,' Rochelle said, 'this is my fault.'

'No.' Leighton shrugged. 'She was already pissed at me before you came along.'

'She doesn't know she's living.'

'None of us do,' Leighton said. 'C'mon, I'll help you make up the bed.'

41

Doug Wilder sighed as he stepped out of his bright orange van. It was a hot afternoon and he had spent the first half of it repairing a burst drainage pipe at the back of a local shopping mall. He had been working for the San Diego Environmental Services, in the commercial drainage section, for just over twelve years and he still enjoyed the work. Some of his buddies from the bowling team liked to poke fun at his job – up to his knees in shit – but Doug didn't view it like that. He had his own reliable transport, visited different places every day, and generally fixed any problem he encountered. He figured that his job was better than being cooped up in some damned office. This afternoon he had driven out of the city in response to a number of complaints about the stink of sewage coming from the side of Barney's Bar 'n' Grill, in the town of Lakehead.

There were various possibilities that might explain the situation. Over the previous decade, Doug had encountered kitchen staff in many establishments who threw food waste out with their general waste. As a consequence, an area could very quickly become a regular feeding ground for rats, cockroaches and all the rest of it. Most locals didn't mind the critters half as much as the smell. Doug was a firm believer that there were few things more offensive than the aroma of spoiled meat that's been fermenting for a few days in the Californian sun. However, in recent years, more food waste was heading to human and animal shelters rather than being left to rot. That made things a little better. Doug reckoned if the trend continued, alongside recycling, refuse collection would end up being a pretty clean and easy occupation. Then the boys on the bowling team wouldn't be laughing so loudly.

Luckily for the locals, he tended to check out these situations in the evening – when the streets were almost always quieter, and the drains could be purged of any offensive matter without spoiling everyone's lunch.

Over the past six months, a number of complaints had been made about the stench coming from the back of Barney's Bar 'n' Grill. Most of the allegations insinuated that Barney Edwards – the proprietor – must be throwing rotting meat into his waste bins, or perhaps even flushing it down his toilets.

Initially, Doug was willing to accept the allegations because even as he crossed the parking lot he could identify a faint, sickly whiff of the aroma the locals had complained about.

It smelled sweet and rotten, a little like a pumpkin that's been left out too long after Halloween.

However, despite the pervasive smell hanging in the air like an unpleasant fog, Doug was unable to locate the source. He wandered around the industrial bins at the back of Barney's without success. It was not coming from the bins nor the building; the waste pipes were running freely, and there were no unpleasant aromas in the toilets – other than the normal reek of shit. Even the storm drains on the road out front were clear and dry of anything other than the occasional lizard.

Eventually, having paced around the area for half an hour, Doug had a moment of inspiration. He looked at the six-foot-high wooden fence that separated the small area at the back of Barney's and the adjacent property, and he climbed up onto it, his feet sliding as he scrambled his way up. That was when he found himself looking into the deserted parking lot of the Sanderson Clinic. From this position, leaning across the barrier, he could confidently state that this was where the foul, gassy smell was definitely stronger.

42

Leighton pulled up thirty feet away from the small house on Thorn Road. This was a residential area to the east of the city, where people lived in small, neat spaces and had little to do with each other. The smooth grey road stretched for half a mile, linking two larger developments, and was lined with small single-storey homes on both sides.

Although he switched off the car engine, Leighton kept the air conditioning running. He knew it wouldn't feel as cool inside without the car running, but at least the fan would keep the air moving. After rechecking the house number, Leighton slid down in his seat, pulled out his cell phone and punched in a number. Within a few seconds, a cheery sounding young woman answered.

'Hi,' Leighton said, 'my name is Michael Stanton. I'd like to order a House Special pizza to be delivered to 311a Thorn Road.' Leighton nodded. 'Yeah, twelve-inch, traditional crust please.' Having completed the call, Leighton got out of his car and wandered away from it until he found a house with an empty drive. He walked up to the porch and rang the doorbell. As he'd suspected, nobody was home. If there had been anybody in the house, Leighton would simply have claimed to be lost, looking for instructions on how to get back to Oceanside Boulevard. Having confirmed the place was empty, Leighton sat down on a small swing seat on the porch. From this position, he could watch Stanton's house, which was farther down the street. The seat gave him a clear view whilst also allowing him to blend in.

After twenty minutes, a small red motorbike groaned to a stop outside Stanton's house. Leighton watched as the delivery driver took a flat container from the heated box on the rear of the bike. He approached the front door and rang the bell.

The door was opened by a frowning man in his late thirties. Leighton felt a surge of adrenaline as he got his first view of the potential killer. Stanton spoke to the delivery man for a moment then emphatically shook his head and closed the door. The delivery driver kicked at the ground and returned to the waiting motorbike. After locking the pizza back in the insulated box, he climbed on his bike and drove off.

Within a few minutes Stanton appeared. He was too far away for Leighton to see if he looked rattled, but he figured he would be. If he really was a killer, he would be concerned about random deliveries showing up at his house, interrupting whatever he was up to in there. A few minutes later, Stanton came out of the house, got into his car, and drove off.

Leighton waited for a few moments before returning to his car. He climbed in and opened the glove box. Taking out a pair of bone coloured latex gloves, he stretched them twice and put them on. He then reached into the back seat and grabbed a small red back pack, which has once belonged to a ten year old Annie - until she moved on to more fashionable accessories.

As he hurried out of his car, Leighton checked all around before approaching Stanton's house. Stepping cautiously around the side of the house, he found himself on a neat terrace.

He tried the glass patio door; to check if it was locked. It wouldn't be a major problem if it was: Leighton had spent more than two decades getting into locked cars and therefore carried a small set of metal picks in his wallet. This set was little more than a selection of tiny hooks, but thankfully it wasn't required; the sliding door was unlocked. Leighton slid it open and exhaled a breath he hadn't realised he was holding.

Before he stepped into the house, Leighton pulled a pair of sky blue shoe covers from the side pocket of his back pack and stretched them over his loafers. He then stepped across the door frame and into Stanton's home.

Inside the house was silent. Moving forwards, Leighton discovered that the patio led into a basic living area – and yet there was little, if any, sign of life.

As he crept into the hallway, Leighton discovered a black canvas holdall sitting close to the front door. Leighton stepped softly toward it and crouched down. At that moment, a car groaned past outside and Leighton froze. He cocked his head, listening for an increase in volume. Thankfully the sound faded away, and Leighton let out his breath. Returning his attention to the object before him, he gripped the zipper and opened the bag. Upon discovering the neatly arranged contents, Leighton immediately understood the purpose of the holdall. There was a glossy map of Black Mountain Open Space Park and a portable stove, along with some torches, snap-lights, flares, and various emergency ration packs. This was clearly a bug-out bag for when things became too hot for Stanton. Leighton glanced at the map and wondered if this location was somewhere that Stanton already knew.

Leighton stood up and walked cautiously into the remaining three rooms. The kitchen was small and tidy, the bedroom looked almost unused, but it was the third room that interested him. There was nothing in the white space other than a desk and chair, and a single shelf on the wall. The shelf was empty with the exception of two small items, and had it not been for one of the items, Leighton would have walked away. Something on the shelf had caught his eye. As he moved toward it, he was unsure of what he was looking at. It seemed at first like a large jewel, but as he got nearer he realised exactly what it was.

When he first met Rochelle, she had told him that Sarah had stolen a tin of cherry lip gloss that had been in the pocket of her jacket. This had stuck in Leighton's memory because his daughter had once had a small tin like that, only Annie's had been watermelon flavoured.

And now, sitting on the shelf, in the house of a convicted killer and current murder suspect, was a tin just like the one Rochelle had lost. Unslinging his back pack, Leighton reached into it and took out a digital camera and a small white plastic ruler. He carefully placed the ruler on the shelf in front of the lip gloss and photographed both items.

Leighton kept the camera in his hand as he crept into the bathroom and glanced around. The shower cabinet was covered in fresh droplets of water, suggesting it had been used recently. Above the small wash basin was a steel medicine cabinet. He opened the mirrored door and found the cabinet contained nothing more than some mouthwash, a nailbrush and a matchbox. Picking up the box, Leighton heard a dry rattle, like the sound of dead bugs, as the contents moved inside. He took a breath and used his fingertip to slide open the small drawer to reveal five teeth. The spiked roots of some of them were still stained by faded blood.

Leighton raised the camera again and took several photographs of the box of teeth. It was then that a rumbling noise from outside caught his attention. This time, when he heard the loud sound of an approaching car, Leighton knew it was the homeowner returning.

'Shit,' he whispered. His hands trembled as he returned the box to the cabinet. He closed it and left the bathroom. As he crossed the hallway he saw the outline of a figure at the mottled glass window of the door. He side-stepped back, into the living room.

He slipped out the way he came – through the patio door – and scrambled over the wall into the adjacent property. He waited there, crouched in some stranger's yard, for several minutes. When Leighton believed enough time had passed, he nonchalantly left the garden of the neighbouring house, and walked purposefully along the street to where his car was parked. Moving briskly, he peeled off the gloves and removed the shoe covers, which he stuffed into a trouser pocket. As Leighton neared the car, he felt a sense of foreboding; perhaps that was why he hadn't turned around to look back, over his shoulder, at the house he had just left. If he had, he would undoubtedly have been unsettled by the figure watching him from the patio window; perhaps more unsettling was the fact that the figure was smiling.

Clambering back into his car, Leighton felt empowered, yet helpless. If he called the station, it was unlikely they would follow it up. Given that he was on suspension, he could be charged with trespass for being in the house, and he could easily end up spending a night or two in the cells. That would take him out of the picture entirely, and Stanton would be able to continue his mission. Yet, he had evidence: the photographs would be enough to justify a visit from Slater and Goza.

Turning the key to start the ignition, Leighton made his decision. He would speak to Rochelle and figure out how to send an anonymous email with the photographs attached. He just wanted to make sure she was safely at home first.

Unfortunately, she wasn't.

43

The sound of repeated knocking on the door roused Rochelle from where she had been sleeping, curled in a warm knot on her couch. She hadn't meant to fall asleep, but when she returned from Leighton's place she had felt more relaxed than she had in many years. Partly, she told herself, due to the warm bath and soft blankets, but also because of the strange feeling that somebody else cared. When she had first woken up in Leighton's home, it seemed for a few precious moments that her other life – her real life – had simply been a nightmare.

That was why, when she returned home to her shitty little world, she'd crawled into unconsciousness: she wanted to escape back to that state of contentment. As she tumbled into the dark warmth of sleep, she hoped to wake up in Leighton's safe haven.

When she heard the sound of the door, she stumbled from the couch and staggered unsteadily, as if the entire apartment was at sea, to answer it.

She fumbled for the lock and then opened the door, expecting to see Leighton's earnest face. She was mistaken.

'Oh shit,' she said as she tried to the slam the door shut again. Unfortunately, she was too slow.

44

Pulling up outside Rochelle's modest home, Leighton glanced at the closed shutters. He checked the time: 6.45pm. That was when he felt a sense of unease begin to uncurl in his guts like an awakening beast. He climbed out of his car and locked the door.

Moving tentatively to Rochelle's front door, Leighton glanced around at the neighbouring windows, most of which had open shutters. He reassured himself that Rochelle's work involved nights, so it was likely that she would only recently have woken, if at all. After ringing the doorbell and getting no response, Leighton tried the door handle and found that the apartment was unlocked.

'Hey,' he called as the door swung inwards, 'Rochelle, are you in there?'

Leighton stepped into someone else's home for the second time that day. The apartment didn't just look messy, it looked like the scene of a fight.

As he wandered back to the door, Leighton noticed something even more alarming.

There were a couple of drops of what appeared to be blood on the white walls of the hallway. Leighton shuddered and began to panic. If Rochelle had been abducted, she was in real danger, possibly dead already.

He staggered out of the apartment to his car and leaned on the hood, breathing in gulps of air. He had to get back to Stanton and confront the bastard. Whether that placed him in danger or not was no longer important.

The house on Thorn Road was shrouded in the long shadows of the early evening when Leighton returned. Thanks to the low illumination of nearby homes, he could see the saloon car was missing from Stanton's drive. He parked his car across the drive, no longer concerned about stealth. His emotions were too raw.

In a moment of anger and frustration, Leighton ran up to the front door and kicked it. The door did not shift. He tried barging it with his shoulder, but the lack of movement suggested it had some type of deadbolt on the other side. He hurried around to the rear of the house and grabbed the handle of the patio door. It too was locked, but Leighton had no patience for lock picking this time. Picking up the steel patio table, he threw it at the large rectangle of glass. It imploded with a deafening bang. Somewhere, nearby, a car alarm began to sound.

Leighton hurried into the dark house. As he suspected, the black holdall was missing from the front door, suggesting that Stanton was long gone and would not be returning to the house tonight. .

Knowing it was only a matter of time before a concerned neighbour heard the alarm and called the cops, Leighton moved quickly from room to room looking for anything that might help him figure out if Rochelle had been inside the place. Thankfully, there was no sign that Rochelle or any other girl had been there. –.

It was then that Leighton remembered the map that had been in the bug-out bag. If Stanton was panicking, and feeling like the net was tightening, he would need to get off the grid. The trails around Black Mountain Park were the perfect place to do that. It was a large area, but Leighton suspected he knew exactly which part Stanton was heading to.

45

As Leighton drove into the dusty landscape of the Black Mountain Canyon, darkness was beginning to fall, and Leighton knew his theory was nothing more than that. With each passing moment it seemed increasingly unlikely that he would locate Stanton. The road was uneven, which caused the car to bounce around and skid on the loose rocks. Since the closure of the mines, the paths around the area were only used by hikers accessing some of the walking trails. This meant Leighton was trying to look out for nothing more obvious than some flattened bushes, in an area of several square miles.

Having looped around twice he was almost ready to give up, when his headlights picked up a glinting metal bumper: Stanton's beige car abandoned off to one side of the mountain track. Had it been an hour later he would never have noticed the car, which blended almost seamlessly with the arid landscape. As he drew close to it, Leighton wondered if its capacity for camouflage had been the reason for Stanton's choice of car. A beige coloured car on a dusty road would be almost impossible to spot from land or air. Leighton also noticed that the car's licence plate had been freshly ripped off. It was a clever move. In a couple of months, the windows would crack, and the sun would scorch away the paint, making the vehicle almost unidentifiable – though the fact it was left-hand drive made it slightly more noticeable. It seemed that the killer was always, both literally and figuratively, a number of steps ahead of his pursuers.

Leighton pulled over a few yards ahead of the other vehicle. Climbing out cautiously, he surveyed the landscape. It was unlikely that Stanton would want to be out in the open for any length of time, but his bug-out bag had provided Leighton with a significant clue to where he was heading. The boxes of highway flares would be useless for anyone on the run in open country. Even if they were hiding out in a barn, or some other outhouse, the bright glow of a burning flare would signal their presence like a shrieking alarm. The only way Stanton could use them without fear of being seen, is if he were inside a windowless building or deep in a cellar. There were few buildings and no cellars on Black Mountain, but there was a large and disused arsenic mine.

Scrambling down the dwindling track, Leighton spotted a yellow warning sign, indicating that the mine up ahead was dangerous. By the look of the dented sign, somebody had been using it for handgun target practice. A few feet beyond the sign was the black entrance to the disused mines. The curved shape of it reminded Leighton of a train tunnel or a gravestone.

46

Crossing the parking lot of the Sanderson Clinic, Doug Wilder let his nose guide him. He walked in overlapping circles like a drunk trying to get home. Occasionally he would stop and close his eyes, as if he were a mystic, attempting to communicate with the spirit world.

In recent years there had been a real boom in different gadgets, with all sorts of gas sensors to help with locating the source of smells, but Doug didn't have any time for that kind of thing. The way he saw it, if you couldn't smell shit, you had no business working in sanitary and waste management. It would be like being a chef with no sense of taste.

As he engaged in his business, Doug concluded that the smell did not actually seem to be emanating from the square building of the clinic itself. He slowly followed the trail to the rear of the building, where there was a square industrial trash can. A glimpse inside revealed it to be empty – other than some old mannequin parts and a couple of bent walking sticks. Yet the stench remained just as intense in this location. It simply didn't make sense.

Doug scratched his head and was struck by a moment of inspiration. He grabbed the large container by the handle and pulled it. It took a fair degree of effort, but eventually the large castors, which had not moved for eighteen months, began to turn. As Doug pulled, the large trash can slowly shifted toward him. Eventually he'd managed to drag the container several feet away from its original location. The momentum made it difficult to stop, but eventually it did. Doug wandered over to where the container had once sat; it was here that he found the previously concealed manhole cover.

Crouching above the large metal disc, Doug confirmed that the stench was rich and undeniably present. Whatever was decaying beneath the manhole cover was unlikely to be a pile of rotten hamburgers.

He stood up and pulled his cell phone from his trousers. He punched in the numbers and held the phone to his ear.

'Hi, yeah, sheriff's department please – I think I've discovered some human remains.'

47

Leighton scrambled into the mouth of the mine, and allowed his eyes to adjust to the infinite gloom of the deep tunnel. Taking a pen-sized Maglite torch from his pocket, he switched it on and pointed it downwards where it illuminated the path ahead with a narrow cone of light.

The rough passage was the colour of rust and stretched deep into the hillside. It appeared to Leighton as if the tunnel had once carried mine carts. The dark, twin lines of the steel rails remained in place, but the intermittent wooden sleepers had long since crumbled to orange dust.

Stepping tentatively deeper into the darkness of the mineshaft, Leighton instinctively removed his pistol from the holster on his belt. He gripped it in one hand, whilst in the other he held the thin Maglite torch like a magician's wand. He was surprised to find the temperature inside warmer than he'd expected. Perhaps a fugitive could survive down here for a long time, if they were prepared, and it seemed Stanton had been.

As he moved deeper into the dripping darkness, Leighton's attention was caught by something glinting on the ground. Directing the torchlight toward it, Leighton found the source of the reflection to be a torn foil wrapper from a snap-light. This confirmed that his instincts had been correct – Stanton had passed through here. That fact both reassured and unsettled Leighton in equal measure.

Leighton crept further along the narrow tunnel, unaware that, back in his abandoned car, his cell phone was vibrating angrily on the dashboard. It buzzed and trembled and eventually slipped off, landing on the carpeted floor.

Moving cautiously through the airless darkness of the chamber, Leighton found the sound of steps to be too loud. He tried stepping lightly, but the uneven surface demanded that he make solid steps to stay upright.

Leighton walked on through the darkness for ten more minutes, before the narrow tunnel widened into a more open area. As he shone the beam around, he discovered the space was roughly twenty feet across and circular. One side feature a curved, scarred wall of orange coloured stone and on the opposite side was a lip of rock, which Leighton almost stepped over. Luckily, he'd shone his torch on it and discovered that the rock fell away on the other side, dangerously tumbling into darkness. It was clear he would have to be careful if he wanted to get out of the place alive.

Turning around, he directed the torchlight back the way he had come. It was then that a sudden blow crashed down upon his right shoulder. The gun and torch both tumbled out of his hands, as the same object smashed sideways into his face. In the chaos of the violence Leighton fell to the ground, where fragments of rock stuck in his hands and knees.

Leighton felt the presence of the man before he saw him; Stanton was hidden in the shadows of the cavern, pointing a pistol directly at him.

'Well, what a regular boy scout you are,' Stanton said from the darkness.

'It's over,' Leighton said breathlessly, 'I'm taking you back.' He grunted as he got unsteadily to his feet.

'Don't be so clichéd. I love your arrogance by the way,' he said. 'You creep in here, like some part-time private investigator, with your pistol and your toy torch, and you honestly think you can take me in.'

'If I found you, others will too.'

'Do you really think you found me by chance? A washed-up meter maid like you?' Stanton laughed.

'I still found you, didn't I?' Leighton asked in a dry whisper.

'Oh, come on, I led you here, Officer. That's why I left a big fucking map right there in my bag. I practically left a sign saying "look in here". Admittedly, I wasn't sure how long it would take, but, thankfully, you're an eager beaver, and I'll get back to my comfy bed soon enough.'

'That place on Thorn Road will be crawling with cops by now.'

'Oh, I doubt that very much,' Stanton said.

'I found the box of teeth in your house. I called it in.'

As Leighton's eyes adjusted he could see the figure more clearly.

'Lucky you. But you should know that those teeth do not belong to any of those poor women.'

'You mean, the women you murdered. Where's Rochelle?'

'Who? Oh, you mean one of the girls. I don't ask their names.'

Leighton let out a raging guttural sob.

'You sound like you're becoming a little unhinged, Officer.'

'Maybe I am,' Leighton said, shaking his head. 'But at least I know who I am, unlike you … Dale.'

There was a hesitation before, eventually, the voice spoke again.

'My name is Michael Stanton.'

'I know you'd like to believe that,' Leighton said quietly. 'I understand how it must have been for you losing Veronica – the first girl you ever loved. You must have wanted Stanton to get a death sentence for that. And yet he got less than two decades. All those years you spent in town, waiting for a chance to take revenge, and then he showed up.'

'That's not true – I'm Stanton.' This time his voice sounded rattled.

'Michael Stanton was right handed, and he only ever drove one car – his father's Duster. But that car you drove here is left-hand drive. The same as the car used to abduct Sarah Kline from the Beach House Café. The same as all three cars ever registered to Dale Sanderson.'

'Only a sad little traffic cop would care about something like that.'

'Did it seem like fate when the Parole Board contacted your clinic asking if you would provide work for somebody who had served their time – repaid their debt? Nobody in Lakehead would touch him, but you had a plan, didn't you? What set you off?"

Something shifted in the younger man's expression. He looked like a different person, and then he spoke. 'He never repaid his debt, not after he took her life.'

'Like you took his?'

'He fucking deserved it,' Sanderson growled, his voice suddenly sounding less controlled.

'So, what about the others, the ones who came after him, did they deserve it too?'

'Maybe. They were all hookers. They looked like Veronica. I couldn't stand to think of her out there letting all those men touch her. Nobody will shed tears for them.'

'Look, Dale, the judge will consider your trauma, how your loss triggered this madness. It could help your case.'

'You think Stanton was the first?' Sanderson laughed obnoxiously. 'I pity you, sincerely; he just gave me a reason, gave me the confidence to step up.'

'Then who was the first? Come on, unburden yourself.'

'Smudge, the family cat. My mother adored the creature more than me. So, when I was eleven years old, I threw it in the chest freezer that we kept in the garage. Then I sat on the lid, listening. There was meowing and all sorts of crazy scratching for a while … then nothing. Later on, I took it out. It had pissed all over the food, but by then it was yellow ice.'

'What did you do?'

'I put it in my backpack. I told my weeping mother I was going out to look for Smudge. She even gave me a hug because she thought I was upset. Stupid bitch. I forgot about that incident until this afternoon when I encountered your friend, Detective Slater.'

'I don't know who you mean,' Leighton said, but he hesitated too long to sound convincing.

'No? He seemed to know all about you. I'd even say he seemed to have some kind of problem with you. Called you a looney. That's why I thought it would be so clever to kill you with his gun. In fact, when I get back, I'm going to plant it on him – alongside his suicide note confessing to your murder. Might even dump him in your home to make it more convincing.'

The possibility of Dale Sanderson finding Leighton's home – and possibly Annie – horrified him.

'You don't know where I live,' he said, hoping that was true.

'Not yet, but a good lawman like you is almost certainly going to have a driving licence on him.'

'I don't,' Leighton lied.

'Hmm.' Dale sounded intrigued. 'You got something at home you don't want me to find? A wife maybe?'

'My wife died years ago,' Leighton said, his voice tinged with genuine sadness.

'Well, it should be fine to leave Slater in your house.'

'Nobody will believe that he killed me.'

'Well, when I add your blood to the soles of his shoes it will add a degree of credibility.'

'They will find you,' Leighton said. 'You do realise that?'

Sanderson laughed, his teeth glinting in the darkness. 'Who exactly is going to find me? This is America: people like me do what we want and rarely get caught.'

'Most get caught.'

'That's what you want to believe. Whores, runaways, hitch-hikers, they all vanish every day, and the public believes there are only a handful of us out there. Nice fantasy! Whilst the public crawl around in their little lives, of fast food, retail therapy and cable TV, real people like me do what we want. I won't be caught, and your body will never be found.'

'Hikers come up here all the time,' Leighton said defiantly.

'Maybe, but the place is being blocked off soon, it's too toxic. So, I doubt your body will ever be discovered; even if it is, Slater will be blamed. You see, that's why I need you to fill a container with some of your blood.'

'But, I want to know something, about the teeth; about the girls.'

''What about them?'

'Why them?'

'You really want to know? You're not just stalling for time?'

'I really want to know, sincerely,' Leighton said.

'Once Stanton was released, I gave him the job and I killed him. It was easy, he was just a shell of a man – I guess the guilt did that to him. Anyway, I did it one night whilst he was mopping the clinic. Made an awful mess, so I wrapped him in shrink-wrap and dropped him into a manhole in the parking lot. After he was down there, I burst open his locker. I had to get rid of his stuff to make it seem like he'd moved on. Would you believe he'd actually kept the ring he'd bought for Veronica, and her little tooth – kept them all those years? I found them in his locker along with his wallet. Fucking loser! Anyway, he was gone, but I still kept thinking about Ronny and how it should have been me, if anyone, who took her life. But after I'd got rid of him, I had his glasses and his wallet, and the keys to his house.'

'So, you stole Stanton's identity and went looking for girls who looked like her. You stole their lives,' Leighton said.

'That's how you view it, Detective. But to be honest, there wasn't much life to steal. I saved them. Anyway, it was Stanton's fault.'

'But, Dale, these aren't Stanton's crimes, they're are yours.'

'Only if I'm caught.'

'Where are the girls' teeth?'

Stanton grinned in the shadows and directed his torch beam to his mouth. 'They're right here,' he said, and he ran his tongue across the pink dental plate in his lower jaw. 'I had to pull out my own to make room for them. Made this little plate myself. I'd been making them for years in the clinic, so when I found Veronica's tooth, I knew what to do with it. I even filed down one of my own and gave it to Ronny's mother; she thinks she has part of her daughter back, she even wears it in a locket around her neck, stupid old bitch! But my way is better: Ronny lives in me, they all live in me. I can taste them forever. Got four little teeth in here so far. I was hoping for more, but you interrupted my work. Still, when I move on to my next city, I'm going to collect an upper set too. What do you think?'

'I think you need help,' Leighton said, trying to mask his horror with a tone of sympathy.

'Maybe, but now that you know how dangerous I am, I'd like the blood I spoke about earlier.' Sanderson reached into his jacket and produced a clear plastic jar, which he threw at Leighton. He directed his torch beam to where the container had landed at Leighton's feet.

'Fill it up,' Sanderson screamed.

'From where?' Leighton asked in a dry whisper.

'Here,' Sanderson said, and fired the pistol. A bright flash illuminated the cave, and the bullet hit Leighton in his left arm. The force of the gunshot threw him backwards against the coarse cave wall. He stumbled against the crumbling surface but somehow managed to stay upright. The momentary numbness of his injury was quickly replaced by a scorching pain that ripped along his bleeding bicep.

The deafening noise echoed through the vast rock chamber, causing a high-pitched ringing in Leighton's ears. However, the noise gave Leighton a momentary advantage, and he used it.

In the chaos following the gunshot, Leighton's functioning hand found his steel baton on the rear of his belt. He used the tip of his thumb to pop the press stud on the webbing holder. Leighton gripped the rubber coating and slid the rod from his trouser belt. With a practised move, he flicked his wrist and the metal rod extended – its slick click was lost in the whining noise. In the gloom, Sanderson, who thought that Leighton was looking for a weapon, decided it would be easier to take a step closer, shoot him directly in the face, and collect the blood himself.

As he approached Leighton, the wounded officer swung his baton upwards and knocked the torch from Sanderson's hand. It flashed like a strobe as it whirled through the air then landed on the ground, casting a bright triangle of light on the cave floor. In a moment of rage, Sanderson fired his gun desperately into the darkness. Both bullets missed Leighton, who had leapt to one side. Instead of killing the detective, Sanderson's wasted gunshots betrayed his location. Leighton's steel baton swung down, smashing Sanderson's wrist and sending his gun into the blackness of the cave. Sanderson screamed but was unable to see his weapon on the ground. In desperation, he leapt for the torch.

Leighton knew if Sanderson reached the torch and found the gun, he would have no chance of surviving. He threw himself toward Sanderson, who turned and grabbed Leighton, his thumb digging into the hot, wet wound in Leighton's arm. The searing pain almost caused him to pass out, but his need to survive was strong.

'Help!' Leighton shouted.

'Nobody's coming for you,' Sanderson sneered. 'You're just as disposable as all those stupid bitches.'

But at that moment, the distant banshee wail of a police siren echoed through the dark chamber. Leighton couldn't see Sanderson's face, but he sensed that his expression was one of fear.

Leighton seized the moment: he broke his arm free and brought his clenched fist, gripping the fat end of the steel baton, down in a hammer blow on Sanderson's contorted face. There was an audible crack as his nose broke; Leighton felt a flood of hot liquid drench his chest. His grip lessened but Sanderson still held fast. Leighton smashed his fist again. The second blow to his face caused something to burst from Sanderson's broken jaw, and he stumbled backwards. Leighton brought the baton forward in a low, wide arc. The force with which he hit Sanderson's lower leg was great enough to send him staggering off to one side. As his fractured leg crumpled beneath him, Sanderson tripped and fell into darkness.

Leighton groaned in agony as he scrambled over the coarse ground to where the abandoned torch lay. Grasping it with his good hand, he limped to the rocky edge and looked down to where Dale Sanderson was thrashing around in a pool of orange liquid. His frantic motions were more than those of someone trapped in deep water. Sanderson's blood streaked mouth was slowly opening and closing, like that of a dying fish. Leighton realised that the concentration of arsenic in the water must have been strong enough to poison the man. Sanderson made a desperate flapping attempt to reach the edge of the pool, before calling out in a croaky retching groan. As the torchlight circled around him like a circus spotlight, he eventually rolled over, before settling face-first in the pool of toxic liquid. Although he was unable to appreciate the irony of his situation, Sanderson's final moments, left, suspended in liquid, were much like those of Jenna Dodds.

Leighton rolled onto his back and tried to concentrate on breathing.

48

The setting sun cast an orange glow over Black Mountain as Leighton Jones stumbled unsteadily out of the mine entrance – the blood from the bullet wound in his arm had soaked his shirt to the point that the entire sleeve appeared black. As he moved unsteadily down the dusty path to his car he found himself surrounded by a crowd of reporters who were jostling uneasily with the arriving police. It was clear to Leighton, from the number of reporters and their proximity, that they had arrived at the dusty location first, and were dominating the territory.

Leighton smiled grimly as he held up his functioning hand to shield his eyes: not from the descending sun, but from the bright spotlights that were fastened to the numerous shoulder-mounted cameras. The media had shown up in record time and reporters were already gathering at the edge of the flimsy police cordon. Leighton was initially surprised to see that there was only one cruiser, with two officers trying to maintain the tenuous boundary, but the sound of sirens was swelling over the city, suggesting that it wouldn't be long before the place was crawling with cops – possibly SWAT teams too.

Somebody called out to him from the bustling crowd of reporters. Usually, Leighton would ignore any such media activity around the periphery of a crime scene, but it didn't anger him; they all had a job to do – news teams included. In any case, this would be the last crime scene he would attend, now Gretsch had finally got his head on a plate.

As he limped in the direction of his car, a reporter called out again to Leighton, but he kept on moving without turning around.

'Officer Jones, can you tell us anything about the owner of the house on Thorn Road?'

'Was that the home of The Dentist?' someone else asked.

'Come on, Officer, we just want to let the public know what's going on,' another reporter shouted.

At that moment, a strange expression appeared on Leighton's face. He paused, and then turned around, limping back to the throng of reporters. Microphones were thrust toward him like giant match heads, and camera lenses appeared over the shoulders of reporters. Leighton leaned toward the nearest microphone.

'Is this thing on?' he asked in a rasping voice.

A reporter nodded enthusiastically.

Leighton looked down the lens of the nearest camera, cleared his throat and spoke slowly and deliberately.

'My name is Officer Leighton Jones of Oceanside Police Department. This evening, I followed a credible lead to an address, where I discovered a number of pieces of evidence suggesting the resident was indeed the serial murderer known as The Dentist. The evidence subsequently led me to this location, where the suspect was hiding out in a disused mine.'

Leighton paused and adjusted his clearly painful arm.

'I attempted to apprehend the suspect; however, he fired at me wounding my arm. Therefore, I was required to use force to defend myself. Unfortunately, the suspect died during the struggle.'

There was a pause, during which time Leighton had to blink against the flutter of camera flashes. This gave him time to formulate exactly what he wanted to say.

'It would be unfair of me to take full credit for this result. I want to state clearly, and on the record, that I followed this line of enquiry on the express instruction of my superior officer – Captain Gretsch of Oceanside PD. He trusted my instincts on this case and advised me that public safety was his greatest priority.'

'Sounds like quite a guy,' one of the reporters called out.

'Oh, he is,' Leighton continued. 'Earlier this month, one of my colleagues – a loyal highway patrolman named Daniel Clarke –

found out that his father was seriously ill. Captain Gretsch demonstrated both his empathy and consideration for the officers in his care, by granting him six weeks paid leave. These are the kind of wise and supportive decisions we see from our captain all the time. Maybe, once in a while, they need to be shared and reported. Now, if you'll excuse me, I need to find a big Band-Aid. Thank you very much.'

'Thank you, Officer,' the reporter said.

Before Leighton approached an awaiting paramedic, he went back to the reporter.

'Hey, how come you guys knew to come out here anyway?' he asked.

'An anonymous phone call from some woman. She told us that a lone wolf cop was out here, taking on The Dentist.'

'Thanks,' Leighton said with a warm smile.

***

In the small hospital room, in Tri City Medical Centre, Danny was sitting by his father's bedside watching a wall-mounted television. As the news report unfolded, he smiled in disbelief at the screen, whilst gently holding the warm hand of his sedated father.

'You clever bastard, Jonesy,' he said, nodding his head.

***

Annie Jones was sitting on the edge of a bright yellow sun lounger in Lina's parents' garden. She was listening to a Shakira CD whilst painting her toenails bright blue, when Lina rushed through the sliding doors from the house.

'Oh my God, Annie,' she squealed excitedly, 'you really need to come in and see this!'

'See what?' Annie asked.

'Just come,' Lina said, beckoning her toward the house.

'What is it?' Annie said, sounding genuinely confused.

'Your dad is on the news. It's all over the television!'

'What is?'

'They're saying he caught a serial killer. I think he was telling the truth last night.'

Annie dropped the nail lacquer and hurried into the house.

***

Officer Sam Westall was on reception duty at Oceanside Police Station when he heard the commotion from Captain Gretsch's office. The reception desk was twenty feet or so away from Gretsch's office door, and yet the noise was enough to reach him. It sounded like some sort of fight. Sam had only been serving for six months, but even in that short time he had found Gretsch to be the most intimidating of all the captains.

Leaving the desk, he cautiously walked down the corridor to where the four captains' offices were located. The noise coming from Captain Gretsch's suggested some type of argument. He could hear the captain shouting vaguely recognisable expletives.

Sam knocked on the thin wooden door, but there was no answer. Eventually, he summoned the confidence to turn the handle. When he opened the door, he discovered Captain Gretsch, breathing heavily, standing in a room that looked like it had been ransacked. A grey filing cabinet was on the floor, and the entire contents of the Captain's desk – including a photograph of him astride his beloved Harley – had been swept onto the floor.

'Are you okay there, Captain?' Sam asked tentatively.

Gretsch said nothing, but his chest continued to rise and fall.

It was then that Sam noticed the television screen suspended on the office wall. The sound had been switched off, but the picture was showing footage, shot from a circling helicopter, of an area of dry scrubland. The scene was covered with the emergency services. A bright yellow banner scrolled across the bottom of the screen: Breaking news – serial killer caught by Oceanside Police operation.

'Wow!' Sam said. 'Have you seen this, Captain?'

At that point, the captain turned his head to look at the younger officer.

'Get the fuck out of here!' he screamed.

'Yes, sir,' Sam said, and retreated from the room. As he closed the door, he could hear the sound of further items being broken on the other side.

49

Leighton carefully placed the box of groceries outside the door and pressed the buzzer. Nothing happened. He tried again, but the sound of thumping music from the apartment next door was too loud to hear anything. Leighton walked to the nearby door and thumped on it with a balled fist.

Moments later the door opened, revealing a dishevelled young man wearing boxer shorts and backwards baseball cap.

'Turn the music down,' Leighton said.

'Or fucking what?' the young man asked with a menacing frown.

Leighton opened his jacket to show his badge.

'Or … I'll arrest you for a four one five misdemeanour and impound your stereo. Even if you make bail, you'll have to wait thirty days before you'll get your hi-fi back. That's assuming nobody at the station accidently breaks it.'

'Fucking harassment,' the young man sneered then slammed his door, but a moment later the music fell silent.

Leighton pressed the buzzer for a third time.

This time the door opened, and a bleary-eyed Rochelle blinked at Leighton, smiling slowly in recognition. 'Hey, Jonesy, I saw on the news. How did you get over here with a busted arm?'

'I took a cab,' he said. 'First time in about ten years.' Leighton found it hard to conceal his delight at seeing she was safe.

'So, I saw that you got your man,' Rochelle said.

'I thought something bad had happened to you. I stopped by, there was some blood and the place was empty.'

'I cut my finger trying to open a packet of cigarettes with a kitchen knife; I had to rush out for supplies,' Rochelle said. It was a lie, but it was easier than telling Leighton that Billy had shown up again after a year on the run. He was looking for his drugs and had been more than happy to punch his way to finding them. Luckily, Rochelle had managed to get away from him before things had got too ugly.

'Oh, I'm sorry,' Leighton blushed. 'Listen, you could have stayed at mine a little longer.'

'It's cool. I decided to clear out not long after you left. I was scared that the mean girls might come back,' she said, grinning.

'Annie showed up yesterday to apologise; to both of us. I guess she realised I was telling the truth.'

'Glad to hear it. So, what brings you over to Cheapville?'

Leighton shrugged. 'I just wanted to say thanks.'

'For what?' Rochelle frowned.

'Calling the news network and sending them out to me.'

'How did you know it was me?'

'Nobody else cares.'

'Well it's cool. When I hadn't heard from you I tried to call you, and then I figured you were in trouble, so I called the news station.'

'How did you know where I was?' Leighton asked.

'I didn't. I gave them your cell phone number and they said they could use GPS to locate it.'

'Thank God they did.'

Rochelle smiled and shrugged her shoulders. 'You did well. They say on the news that the sick bastard killed Jenna and Danielle too, is that right?'

'Yeah, I'm sorry.'

'You've got nothing to be sorry for. That bastard would have kept going. You saved a lot of lives; made a real difference, Officer Jones.'

'What about you?' Leighton asked.

'What about me?' Rochelle shrugged and leaned on her doorframe.

'I could get you into a programme – no cost.'

Rochelle sighed, and looked at Leighton the way an adult might look at a child.

'Jeez, you're such a kid sometimes.'

'What does that mean?'

'Don't you get it? Not all problems can be fixed, Leighton. Girls like me are different, we don't get a "happy ever after".'

'Why not?'

'Hell knows, maybe we were born bad, or broken; maybe it's payback for some shit we did as kids, or in a past life, or some shit like that.'

'Or,' Leighton said slowly, 'maybe you just made some poor choices when you were too young to know any better. And now you could make some new ones – better ones.'

'Remember you're a fucking cop not a preacher.'

'Look,' Leighton sighed. 'I'm just saying, if you need some help—'

'I don't,' Rochelle said resolutely.

'At any time, give me a call, okay? Some people do care.'

He handed her a small business card and turned to go. Rochelle glanced down at it, and then at Leighton as he walked away.

'Wilson!' she suddenly called after him.

'Huh?' Leighton stopped and turned around.

Rochelle shrugged self-consciously. 'My surname is Wilson. Rochelle Wilson. I just wanted you to know.' Having shared this private information, she vanished inside her apartment, and Leighton – understanding the amount of trust she had revealed – walked to his car with a smile on his face.

Later that afternoon, Leighton decided to build some bridges with Annie. He explained that he needed to take a drive up north, and that he would let Annie take the wheel if she wanted to improve her driving skills. In any case, the injury to his arm meant he had no choice.

After packing some bottles of Coke and some water in a cool bag, Leighton and Annie left Oceanside behind and were soon cruising along beneath the hot Californian sun. They didn't sing any songs together, but they did speak for most of the way and even played I Spy for a couple of miles.

When they arrived in the town of Lakehead, Leighton asked Annie to pull up in the main street. The town looked prettier than Leighton had remembered. He reached into his worn wallet and handed Annie a couple of twenties.

'What's the plan?' she asked.

'I've got to visit someone,' Leighton said, 'but I'll only be twenty minutes or so.'

'Sounds very mysterious. You can tell me, are you a crooked cop dad?'

'Not yet,' Leighton smiled. 'If you want to have a look around the shops, I can meet you at the coffee shop and we can grab some lunch?'

'Shopping and lunch – that sounds sweet.'

'I'll be twenty, maybe thirty, minutes, and then I'll wait for you at the coffee shop, okay?'

'Sure,' Annie said, and climbed out of the car.

Ten minutes later Leighton pulled up beneath the tall palms of the Golden Cross Care Home. This time he hadn't made an appointment. Thankfully, there was an outdoor, water-colour painting class taking place in the garden, and it looked like most of the residents and staff were sprinkled around outside.

As he entered the building for the second time, Leighton found the post-lunch aroma to be less pleasant than it had seemed on his first visit. The smell of stewed beans and boiled meat seemed to cling to the walls. Leighton retraced his steps to the day room, where a solitary resident sat firmly in her chair.

As he approached Eileen Cooper, Leighton noted she was wearing a different expression from the one he remembered. Her look of concern had been replaced by one of defiance. This time the police officer felt no need for pleasantries or introductions.

'You knew, didn't you,' he said flatly. It wasn't a question.

'I had my suspicions,' Mrs Cooper said quietly, but with an air of indifference, 'that was all.'

'They told me that you had weekly visits up until last year. Were those visits from him, from Dale?'

'He was as broken as I was. We comforted each other. I suppose we both felt we were somehow keeping Veronica alive through our conversations.'

'Had he always planned to kill Michael Stanton?'

'I'm really not sure. He certainly talked about it – we both did. But as the release date grew nearer, Dale left me out of his plans. Then he showed up here one evening and told me that he'd given Stanton a job. He was so excited. He told me that he had him where he wanted. I didn't see Dale for several days after that, but when he finally visited, he told me that he had a gift for me. It was Ronny's milk tooth. He said he'd found it in Stanton's locker, along with an old photograph of her from her school yearbook.'

'Is that what made him do it?' Leighton asked. 'Did finding that make him kill Stanton?'

'Possibly. The mind is a fragile thing, Officer Jones.'

'You told me that you often have nightmares in which you see what happened to your daughter.'

'That's true, some things can't be unseen, I'm afraid.'

'What about the parents of those murdered girls, don't you think they will have nightmares now?' Leighton struggled to conceal his anger. 'You could have reported Dale Sanderson and prevented the pain of those girls and their families.'

'We all have a cross to bear. The universe has been cruel to all of us,' Eileen Cooper said, as she deliberately turned away to stare into the complex patterns of the garden area. 'Please go now. I'm tired.'

'Is that it?' Leighton asked. 'No remorse? Nothing?'

Eileen Cooper continued staring at the curled green tongues of the numerous cacti and palms that filled the large gardens of the home. She was quite happy to play the waiting game.

When she turned around, she found that Leighton Jones had thankfully gone; she smiled and breathed a deep sigh of relief.

Then she glanced down.

Arranged on the floor, in a fan shape, were the crime scene images of Sanderson's murder victims: Sarah Klein, Jenna Dodds, Elizabeth Walker, Danielle Millar, and Detective Ryan Slater. The photos ranged from head shots of the deceased – for identification purposes – to magnified images of individual wounds.

Eileen Cooper twisted her head quickly, in an attempt to look away, but it was too late; the images had caught her attention like fishhooks on her eyes. She began calling, angrily, for a nurse who never came. Leighton was also responsible for that.

Five minutes earlier, as he passed through reception, he'd told the nurse at the desk that he had heard an elderly woman calling for assistance in the front gardens. She had consequently rushed outside, leaving Eileen Cooper to her pictures and her guilt.

She eventually, in her rage and distress, tried to twist her body around in the rocking chair to escape the infinite stare of the dead. Unfortunately, her lack of strength in her right side had placed her significantly off balance, and she tumbled from the rocking chair, clattering onto the floor.

Lying with her face touching two of the six-by-eight glossy photographs, of ligature marks on Sarah Klein's throat, Eileen Cooper began to make sobbing, guttural noises, which ironically echoed the final sounds of most of Dale Sanderson's victims.

As Leighton entered the aromatic coffee shop, where Annie was sitting at the counter chatting to Leanne, both women smiled at him. The place smelled of fresh coffee and warm muffins. He joined them, taking a seat at the counter. It was then, for the first time in what seemed like years, that Leighton felt a moment of discernible happiness. Leaving the images with Eileen Cooper had left him strangely unburdened. He had followed the advice of the grief counsellor and, as a result, the case was closed; Danny still had a job and, best of all, his daughter looked relaxed and genuinely pleased to hang out with him for a while. Things, it seemed, were finally looking up.

50

It was two days later when Leighton finally returned home from his drive with Annie, which included an impromptu visit to the rocky mountain splendour of Marshall's Peak, and a night stop at a fairly sumptuous hotel in San Bernardino. Leighton had particularly enjoyed the free breakfast of fresh melon and pineapple; Annie had been more impressed by the heated pool. Throughout the drive back to Oceanside, father and daughter had talked properly for the first time in years. And, perhaps for the first time, Leighton had actually listened. Annie had explained how she was interested in hair and beauty, and that she had never been particularly academic, but explained how she didn't want to take a job that her dad would look down on. Leighton told her that he just wanted her to be happy and, if she wanted to train in hair and beauty, he would support her all the way. As a result of their conversation, Annie had cheerfully agreed to apply to the Oceanside College of Cosmetology, with a view to starting her training the following month. The decision gave them both a much-needed sense of peace. Eventually, they had turned up the radio and sang loudly as they travelled through miles of vineyards and orange orchards. For Leighton Jones, it was one of the happiest moments in his life.

When they arrived back in the city, Annie was desperate to catch up with Lena. Leighton dropped her off on the condition that both girls would come to his house for supper the following evening. Annie had agreed, but only on the condition that the dinner included a couple of pizzas and some tubs of overpriced ice cream. Despite stating that she was pushing her luck, Leighton agreed to his daughter's demands.

Half an hour later, having entered his home carrying a bulging bag of trash from the car, Leighton closed the front door with his foot. He put his burden down and crossed the room to discover that somebody had left a message on his answer machine. He knelt on the floor by the coffee table, lifted the handset and pressed the flashing button. An automated voice told him there was one missed call, then played the message:

'Hey, Jonesy, its Wendy, give me a call at the station when you get this. I'm on until six.'

Leighton stood up and punched the station number into the phone handset, holding it to his ear. As it rang, he wandered into the kitchen where he had placed his trash bag next to the waste paper bin. After three rings, the phone was answered.

'Oceanside Police Station, how may we help you?' asked a cheery voice.

'Wendy?' Leighton said tentatively.

'Yes, who is this?'

'Leighton Jones. What's up?'

'Ah, Jonesy, there was a message left here for you. Give me a second.'

'Couldn't it wait until next week? I don't often get updates at home.'

'Yeah, I know, sorry about that.'

'Hey, its fine, I'm just teasing. What was the call?' Leighton tried to swap the phone to his other hand but winced against the pain in his upper arm. He cradled the phone between one of his shoulders and his ear as he opened the refrigerator and removed a bottle of beer.

'You're the main topic of conversation down here at the station, you know?'

'Yeah?' Leighton frowned.

'Some people are saying that Gretsch knew nothing about your investigation, but he's having to take the credit just to help him move up to chief.'

'Well, I'm just happy to help out such a nice guy,' Leighton chuckled.

'Yeah right. Okay, the message was from a girl,' Wendy continued, 'she was real insistent about speaking to you. I mean *real* insistent, so I told her that you were off duty for the weekend, but she wouldn't let up.'

'What did she say?' Leighton asked.

'She said to tell you that "she's ready". That's all – no name or other words – just "she's ready". Does that make any sense to you?'

'Yes.' Leighton smiled to himself. 'Yes, it does, thank you Wendy.'

'Okay, well that's you updated, Officer. Have a good Sunday night, Jonesy. When you back in the madhouse?'

'Tuesday,' Leighton said.

'Well, I guess I might see you at the coffee machine,' Wendy said, 'if it's a slow shift.'

'Not had one of them in quite a while,' Leighton said, laughing.

'We must all live in hope, Jonesy,' she said, and hung up.

Leighton carried the phone and his bottle of beer out onto his porch, where he pulled out a steel garden chair and sat down. As he took in the dramatic sunset, he held the beer between his knees, twisted off the cap with his right hand and took a sip. It was cold and tasted clean. Taking a deep breath, he allowed himself to inflate, holding on to the breath momentarily, before breathing out and feeling himself relax. It was another trick he had picked up from the grief counselling sessions, that, and focusing on helping to make a positive difference to the lives of those around him. Leighton had never been much of a believer in his ability to influence others, but sometimes the world still had the potential to throw him a curveball.

'She's ready,' he said with a smile.

It was a warm evening and a 747, leaving Oceanside Municipal Airport, whined overhead, leaving a faint white line like a scratch in the orange Californian sky.

Epilogue

By the time he turned his car onto Fenwick Avenue, Leighton had been up and busy for a couple of hours. It had been difficult getting back behind the wheel of his car again, but he had been determined to make this trip. Straight after breakfast he had driven across the city to Oceanside Rehab centre, where he spoke to a relaxed counsellor called David, and made arrangements for Rochelle to enter into a six-week programme. It was, thankfully, a free service, but Leighton had wanted to drop off some money to cover anything she might need during her stay.

He explained to David that he didn't want Rochelle to know, otherwise she might have mistaken Leighton's support for charity – something he felt she would not welcome. However, neither did he want to simply give her the cash – just in case she slipped back into an old habit. He figured he would simply tell her that the centre would provide any clothing or personal items she might need.

Following his visit to the centre, Leighton made a brief trip to the shopping mall just off Vista Way, before heading back to collect Rochelle.

Driving toward her apartment, Leighton was puzzled to see two black and white patrol cars and an ambulance parked at random angles in the street outside it. Some locals – teenagers mainly – were pressing excitedly against the yellow crime scene tape as if they were trying to get into a concert.

Leighton felt his stomach lurch as he pulled the car to a stop and clambered out. Pushing his way through the crowd of eager onlookers, he was jostled until he ducked under the tape and stepped onto the grubby concrete steps that lead to her door. After pulling out his badge, he knocked on the door with a hand that was visibly shaking. It was opened by a patrol officer, who Leighton vaguely recognised.

'Hey, Jonesy, isn't it? I saw you on TV – good work on the Black Mountain ranch shit. What you doing here? I thought they said you were working traffic?'

'Yeah,' Leighton said, and tried to disguise his unease. 'I am. I was just passing and saw the black and whites. What's happened here?'

'A local hooker,' the officer said, glancing over his shoulder to where Rochelle's lifeless body was lying on the kitchen floor. She appeared to be dressed in her best clothing, as if she had wanted to make a good first impression at the rehab centre. 'Looks like she was killed by her addict boyfriend, or pimp. There was a small suitcase half packed on the bed, so we figured she was possibly planning to leave him.'

'How did she die?' Leighton felt as if he had been punched in the stomach.

'A fatal stabbing. Hey, you okay, man?' the rookie asked.

'I had a rough night, I just need a coffee,' Leighton lied. 'Did anyone ID the victim?'

'Sure. She is …' the officer said as he pulled out a notepad from his chest pocket, 'Ms Rochelle Grace Wilson – according to the bills piled around the place. A neighbour said she heard the guy show up, banging on the door, early this morning. She said the victim was a hooker. The guy was apparently yelling about some drugs, and trying to bust the door in.'

'Was the neighbour the one who called it in?' Leighton asked.

'Yeah, when we pulled up outside, the boyfriend was already in the house. The victim was lying there, cold on the kitchen floor, and the guy was sitting next to her, eating a bowl of oatmeal. My partner Marty kicked in the door and warned the guy, but the asshole made a grab for a knife. He told us to stay out of his business or he'd put us in the ground. Thought he was Rambo.

The asshole took three shots in the chest before he went down; he must've been high on some shit.'

'Jeez.' Leighton nodded, trying to avoid looking at Rochelle's lifeless body. 'Anything I can do to help?'

'No, thanks, the lab guys will be here soon, then I guess it's all just waste disposal from here. "Clean the whore off the floor", as they say.'

Leighton paused, half turned to go, and turned back around. 'You married?' he asked the officer.

'What?' The younger man seemed momentarily knocked off balance.

'You got a wife? Girlfriend? I presume you do, right?' Leighton continued.

'Yeah, sure,' the officer said with a shrug of his shoulders.

'You got any kids?' Leighton asked.

'Yeah – two. One of each.' The officer grinned at some memory of his children's craziness.

'Well, that murdered girl, lying back there on the kitchen floor, is someone's daughter. Just as important as your own little princess, maybe even more so, because whilst your kids will grow up in a nice neighbourhood, with loving parents and a happy life, that girl lying on the floor got a shit life at the hands of shit men. So right now, she deserves to be treated with some dignity, probably for the first time in her short fucking life.'

'Jeez,' the officer said, as he looped his thumbs into his belt defensively. 'Preach much?'

Leighton said nothing, just turned and walked back toward the fluttering police tape and the sea of eager onlookers. His hand reached into his jacket pocket for his car keys and found something else. Although it was a tiny, almost imperceptible gesture, his finger touched the small plastic dice and curled around it as if it were the most precious thing in the world.

'Hey,' the young officer called after Leighton from the doorway of the murder scene, 'don't get so worked up about it, Jonesy – she was just another hooker, right? Right?'

As he climbed back into his car, started the engine, and stared through his windshield, Leighton wasn't looking at the crowd of ghouls, or at the flashing lights of the emergency vehicles. He wasn't even looking at the grubby little apartment in which his friend had been cruelly murdered. Instead, Leighton was looking at a different future: one where Rochelle had somehow escaped her confinement and found the life she deserved. He could imagine her, having got cleaned up, living in a neat little house somewhere in Minnesota, where the walnut trees were tall and green, and the air was fresh.

As he used the palm of his hand to wipe the hot tears from his eyes, Leighton deliberately avoided glancing sideways at the bag of neatly pressed and folded clothes, which sat on the passenger seat of his car. They were only clothes after all.

But perhaps more upsetting for him were the two books that he had carefully placed beside the clothes – a cookery book of *Fresh Pasta Sauces for Beginners* and a hardback edition of *The Little House on the Prairie* by Laura Ingalls Wilder.

Leighton, still struggling with the row of painful stitches in his upper arm, grunted as he put the car into gear. He gripped the steering wheel and began to drive slowly out of Fenwick Avenue. He kept his eyes straight ahead as he turned his car away from the street on which Rochelle had lived for a short time and drove off to face another day in Oceanside.

***

Acknowledgments

Heartfelt thanks to Betsy and the team at Bloodhound Books for their commitment and support. Thanks also to Richard Laird for giving me the benefit of his experience in law enforcement.

Lightning Source UK Ltd.
Milton Keynes UK
UKHW011939090719
345866UK00001B/153/P